GARY'S ADVENTURES IN CHESS COUNTRY

BY IGOR SUKHIN

MONGOOSE
Press

Boston

© 2008 Igor Sukhin

Publisher: Mongoose Press
1005 Boylston Street, Suite 324
Newton Highlands, MA 02461
info@mongoosepress.com
www.MongoosePress.com

ISBN: 9780979148224

Library of Congress Control Number: 2008940522

Distributed to the trade by National Book Network
custserv@nbnbooks.com, 800-462-6420
For all other sales inquiries please contact the publisher.

Layout: Semko Semkov
Editorial Consultants: Laurie Boris, Rebecca Carr
Cover Design and illustrations: Creative Center – Bulgaria

First English edition
0 9 8 7 6 5 4 3 2 1

Printed in China

CONTENTS

INTRODUCTION

Anyone can reap benefits from learning chess, but young children often gain the most from the game. Chess provides children the opportunity to learn pattern recognition and critical thinking skills. Practicing basic chess skills motivates them to think, which, in turn, builds nerve connections in the brain.

Social benefits are often reaped as well. The game of chess rewards courage, sportsmanship, and self-control, while allowing children to positively interact with their peers. Chess players who learn to win and lose graciously often make many lifelong friends as a result. Perhaps the greatest social benefit chess can offer is an avenue for earned success, the kind that helps children build the confidence and self-esteem they need to excel in school.

Many parents feel daunted by the prospect of trying to teach their young children to play chess. If you are unsure of how to teach your child the game, fear not. The book you now hold in your hands, Igor Sukhin's *Gary's Adventures in Chess Country*, has been carefully designed to take the intimidation factor out of learning chess. Set in the magical realm of Chess Country, it reads like a children's bedtime story; yet, at the same time, it introduces the game of chess gradually, using stories, puzzles, riddles, and quizzes.

Too often I have seen young students overwhelmed by the task of learning the moves of the chess pieces. If the entire game is presented at once, without time for any review, frustration often results. *Gary's Adventures in Chess Country* continually reinforces what has been learned through its stories and chess problems. By the time your child plays his or her first game, he or she will already have solved dozens of puzzles reinforcing each chess rule. He or she will be able to make chess moves with confidence.

Finally, *Gary's Adventures in Chess Country* is more than just an instruction manual. It is a tool to help you create your own unique chess adventure with your child. It is an invitation to a chess expedition, an exciting journey that just keeps getting better. It is my hope that after reading about the adventures of Gary, Cassie, Riddles, and their friends, your child will embark on his or her own richly rewarding chess adventures.

Susan Polgar
Women's World Champion, 1996-1999

Chapter 1

Sometimes, when you want something interesting to happen to you badly enough, your wish can come true. Or, at least Gary hoped so. His parents were away on a trip and had left Gary with the most boring babysitter in the history of the universe. So he really, really wanted something interesting to happen to him right this very minute! But Gary had no idea he'd end up starring in a magical story. And this is how it happened.

On Sunday morning, the doorbell in Gary's apartment rang. He hoped it was one of his buddies. But Gary opened the door and, instead of one of his friends, he saw a girl in a checkered dress.

"Hello, Gary," the girl said. "My name is Cassie. I have come to take you to Chess Country."

Before Gary could reply, or even ask how she knew his name, his mysterious visitor took him by the hand and led him to a six-seated tricycle parked nearby. Cassie got in front, and Gary made himself comfortable in one of the back seats.

And so the journey began. The tricycle traveled at an unbelievable speed. Cities, forests, and rivers came up and fell behind in the blink of an eye. With his heart pounding in his chest, Gary knew something wonderful and amazing was about to happen. Then Cassie slowed down and stopped the trike in front of a beautiful pavilion that looked like a tower.

"This is the Chess Pavilion," Cassie said. "Here we will have our first lesson."

Outside, a boy about Gary's age was playing. He scowled when he saw Gary and Cassie.

"You're going to learn chess?" he asked with a sneer. "You'll never beat me, no matter how much you practice."

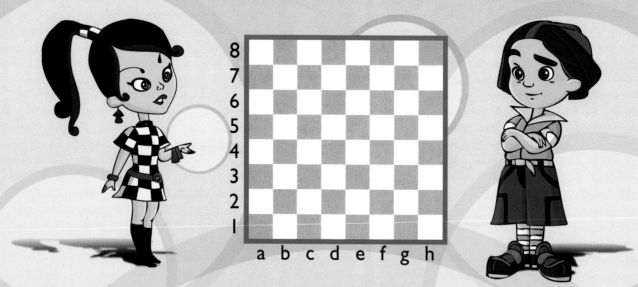

"That's Zug," Cassie said. "Just ignore him. That's how he is to everyone."

Gary followed the girl inside and froze in amazement. On a massive table that gave off soft, pink light, lay a big board with many dark and light squares.

"This is a chessboard, where chess battles are fought," Cassie explained. "The chessboard is divided into equal square pieces. The white ones are called light squares. The black ones are dark squares."

Light squares   **Dark squares**

"Light squares, dark squares," Gary repeated.

Suddenly, the squares on the board quivered and darted off to the ground. Black and white, they began to dance around Cassie and Gary.

"These are my little friends," Cassie said with a smile. "Here in the Chess Pavilion, the squares are magical."

Soon, the squares stopped dancing, and in a flash they were back on the board.

Gary was puzzled. Did that really happen, or was he imagining things? He stepped closer to the board to see what was going on and almost fell, stumbling over something. On the floor he saw a thick notebook, the size of *The Yellow Pages*. Gary picked it up and read from the cover: "Riddles' Pad."

"Oh! This notebook belongs to my friend, Riddles," Cassie said. "It's great that you found it! It's full of jokes, puzzles, and chess exercises. If you read it and try to answer the questions, even a little at a time, it will help you to learn the game of chess. Shall we start?"

Gary nodded, still too surprised by what was happening to speak.

RIDDLES FROM THE PAD

1. Riddles says you'll easily get the point of this question: Point to a dark square and a light square on a chessboard. Which is bigger, dark or light?

2. What shape is the chessboard, square like a piece of bread or round like one of Cassie's tricycle tires?

3. What's bigger: a chestnut, a chess square or a chessboard?

4. What board cannot be used for surfing or skating? (Or ironing!)

5. Find all the chess patterns on this picture.

Chapter 2

"Now let's start our second lesson," Cassie said.

"The game of chess is played by two people who compete against each other," she told Gary. "They are called opponents. The two sit face to face across the board. The chessboard is arranged so that the corner square to the right of each opponent is light. It's easy to remember. Just say to yourself: "Light on the right!"

How should we sit down and set up the board?

HELP GARY

Gary showed Cassie where she should sit. Then he sat across from her, like this:

"The light corner square is on my right," Gary said.

Then Gary noticed that off to the side of the board, there was a tiny house shaped like a cube. The house had carved windows, a very small door, and a fancy-looking porch. On the porch were three brightly colored buttons: a red one with the letter F on it, a blue one with an R, and a green one with a letter D.

Gary was puzzled.

"What is that?" he asked.

"I will explain the house and buttons in a minute," Cassie told him. "First, look at the chessboard. Squares of different colors (light and dark) always switch back and forth. Dark is followed by light, light by dark."

"Any dark and light path of eight squares going from left to right is called a rank," she said. "Look, here is a rank."

Cassie pressed the button that had an R on it.

Precisely at that moment, the door of the cube-house opened and a tiny, smiling creature appeared. He gracefully jumped on the first light square and hopped through the first row of squares to the opposite side of the board. Then he turned around and, just as quickly, ran back to his little house and disappeared inside.

Gary was so surprised, he stumbled sideways, bumping into the chessboard and knocking a few squares to the floor.

"Is that tiny man alive?" he asked, still staring into the little cube house.

"No, he's just a toy," Cassie said, and looked sad for a moment.

But she quickly brightened. "He's our friend, and he's a robot. He just showed you one of the horizontal lines, a rank. There are eight of them altogether. Look! As you move along the ranks, every light square is followed by a dark square."

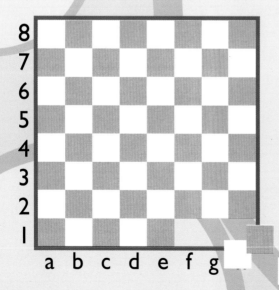

Gary picked up the dropped squares and looked at the board in confusion. **Where did they all go on the board?**

10

Suddenly Gary figured out the answer and, relieved, clapped his hands. When he put the dark and light squares back in their proper places, Cassie cheered, then got back to their lesson.

"You already know what ranks are," she said. "Are you ready to learn the rest of the lines?"

She reached for the button with the F on it.

"Any up and down row that leads across the board from one opponent to the other is called a file," she explained. "Just like with the ranks, there are eight files."

Cassie continued. "And just like with ranks, every dark square is followed by a light one, every light one by a dark one."

The little robot again came out of his house and ran towards the board. He crossed the board from one side to the next, this time going on a file.

As he was running back, he bumped a couple of squares so they piled up on one another.

"Which squares did he move?" Cassie asked.

This time, Gary easily returned the squares to their proper places.

"Bravo," Gary's new friend said as she clapped her hands. "You are learning quickly. Now you are ready to do some riddles from the notebook."

1. Besides putting your bottom on a chair, what's the right way to sit at the chessboard?

2. Ready to show a rank? How many squares does it have?

3. OK, if you're so smart, show all the ranks. How many of them are there?

4. Show a file. (And not a computer file!) How many squares are there?

5. Show all the files. How many of them are there?

6. You won't need a ruler for this one. What's longer: a rank or a file?

7. Think carefully! Could there be 2 dark squares next to each other on a file? What about 2 light ones?

8. If you got the last one, this one will be easy. Could there be 2 dark squares next to each other on a rank? What about 2 light ones?

9. How many light squares are on a file? On a rank?

10. We hope you're not afraid of the dark! How many dark squares are on a file? On a rank?

11. Are there more dark or light squares on a file? What about a rank?

12. Are these ranks and files drawn correctly?

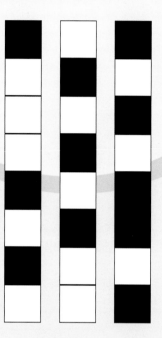

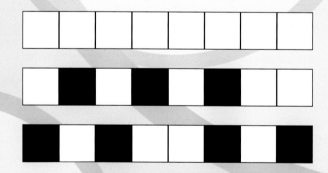

Just then, another boy came into the pavilion. He had a pug nose and large, friendly eyes. Under his arm he carried a long, thin stick.

"Gary, this is Riddles," Cassie said happily. "He will travel with us. He knows a lot of funny chess stories."

"Why are you carrying a stick?" Gary asked.

Riddles looked a little offended at the question. "It's not just a stick; it's a pointer. It will come in handy on our journey."

"It sure will," Cassie agreed. "Now, let's talk about diagonals on the chessboard. A diagonal is a straight chain of squares of the same color that touch each other's corners. Diagonals are slanty like an X and come in different sizes. The shortest ones are only two squares long!"

Riddles waved his pointer and showed the short diagonals.

"There are also two very long diagonals on the chessboard, going all the way from corner to corner," Cassie continued. "One dark, and one light. Each of them has eight squares. Our little friend will show us the big light diagonal."

Gary looked expectantly at the little cube house, and Cassie pushed the bright green button with the letter D on it.

The odd little robot man hurried to the opposite corner of the board and back before disappearing into his tiny house.

"Chess Country is fun," Gary said to Cassie. "And your friends are cool."

Just then, all the squares jumped off the board and danced around Gary. Like snowflakes in a storm they went around, up, and down. It was hard to keep track of them.

Gary couldn't resist; he reached out and caught a bunch of dark squares. When the rest of them returned to the board, one of the dark diagonals was not there.

Gary quickly released the dark squares he was holding, and sighed with relief when they returned to their proper places on the board.

"Now you have seen all the paths of the chessboard: ranks, files, and diagonals," Cassie said. "Next, Riddles will show you the center."

"The center is the four squares in the very middle of the board. Two of which are dark and the other two are light." Riddles said as he pointed. "Now, Gary, it is time for you to solve more of my puzzles."

With that, Riddles opened his notebook.

HELP GARY

1. Maybe you don't have a fancy pointer like Riddles', but you only need your finger to point to a diagonal. How many squares does it have?

2. Show the long dark diagonal. How many squares are there?

3. Here's a riddle for you. Which diagonal is longer: the long light one or the long dark one?

4. Point to one of the shortest diagonals. How many squares are there?

5. Put on your detective cap and find a diagonal that contains 3, 4, 5, 6, and 7 squares. Do the end squares of each diagonal have the same color?

6. Are these diagonals drawn correctly?

7. Point to the center.

8. You can't eat it, but what shape is the center, round like a donut or square like ravioli?

9. How many light squares live in the center? How many dark ones?

10. Are two squares of the same color next to each other in the center?

11. Is this a correct drawing of the center?

15

"OK, I understand everything about the board," Gary said. "But what do you use to play chess?"

"Chess pieces," answered Cassie. "On the chessboard, two armies of chess pieces fight a battle. One of the opponents leads the army of light pieces. They are called White. The other opponent commands the army of dark pieces. They are called Black."

Gary was fascinated. "What are the pieces like?" he asked.

"Our robot friend will show you, if you guess how to ask," Riddles said.

Gary was a bit frustrated at this answer.

"Does he have to talk in riddles?" he wondered.

He leaned over the house-cube and whispered: "Hey, dude, show me the pieces."

There was no response. Then Gary remembered his manners. "Please?"

Still, no answer. Gary tried to open the door, but it didn't budge. What could he do to solve this puzzle? He went around the board, inspecting every inch of the space. Then, next to the house, he discovered another six buttons, with the letters P, N, B, R, Q, and K on them.

These must somehow be related to the pieces, thought Gary. He reached out and pressed the closest button, the one with the letter P on it. Two short figures with round heads appeared on the chessboard: a white one and a black one.

At the same time, the door of the house-cube opened and the tiny robot man appeared on the porch with an explanation:

"These are called Pawns. Each side, Black and White, has eight of them to start the game."

Gary stared for a moment, then pressed the B button. The pawns began to grow; their round heads became pointed and sharp.

Gary rubbed his eyes and blinked a few times. The pieces remained tall and pointy-headed.

"These are the Bishops," the robot man explained. "There are two each, Black and White, to start the game."

Gary continued his investigation, this time pressing the N. The pointed heads of the bishops started to blur again, and this time, they turned into something that looked like horses.

"These are Knights," the little robot continued, "And again, each army gets two apiece."

"Where are the knights? Looks like they got kicked off their horses." Gary muttered. "And why does the button have N for Knight? Doesn't knight start with a K?"

"Yes, the knights had to give up their first letter," Riddles said, "because somebody very important wanted to use it. You will see later."

Gary pressed the button with R on it, and the knights morphed into two massive forms, shaped like towers.

"These are Rooks, white and black, two to a customer," the robot said.

"Some people call them castles," Cassie said. "My name is actually Castle, but my friends call me Cassie."

"Rooks." repeated Gary. He examined the new pieces for a moment, and then pressed the Q button. In a flash, in place of the rooks appeared two beautiful, tall pieces with elegant crowns on their heads.

"These are Queens," the robot told Gary. "Queens are so important that each army only gets one."

"Now, press the last button. What do you think is there?"

Gary shrugged his shoulders, then pushed the button with K, transforming the queens into majestic kings.

"Yes, they are kings!" the robot man confirmed upon seeing Gary's awed look. "So royal and powerful that, like the queens, each army only gets one."

"Wow, they do look royal and powerful," Gary said with admiration.

Gary thought about all the pieces he had just learned.

"Hey, I think I know what important piece took the letter K from the knights!" he exclaimed.

"You are right, a knight can't argue with the king!" the little robot agreed.

He waved his hand and the kings disappeared off the board.

"Are you sure he's a toy?" Gary said to Riddles, as he studied the robot man up close. "I never would have guessed."

"I heard an incredible story about him," Riddles whispered, "that he used to be a dwarf, but he made a witch angry, and she turned him into a toy."

"Is it possible to lift the curse somehow?" Gary asked. He felt so nervous that he almost forgot how to breathe!

"You need to uncover the second secret of these three letters," said Riddles, as he pointed to F, R, and D.

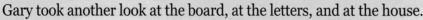

DO YOU REMEMBER THE FIRST SECRET?

"We remember the first secret!" Cassie said. "File begins with F, Rank with R, and Diagonal starts with D!"

"Yeah, the first one is easy. It's the other one that's a mystery to me," Riddles mumbled.

Gary took another look at the board, at the letters, and at the house.

Suddenly, he understood. "Yes! I know! FRD also stands for Fred – his name is Fred!"

A white light flashed in front of Gary's eyes. Suddenly the little robot perked up, and laughing loudly, he bowed before Gary.

"Ho, ho, ho," he bellowed, and started hopping on one foot.

"You are right! My name is Fred! Thank you, Gary! Thank you and…goodbye," said Fred, and then he ran away.

"Where did he go? What's going on?" Gary wondered.

Things were happening so fast.

"You lifted the curse; he is free to go wherever he pleases," Riddles said, laughing. "Oh, he'll be running around for a while now. Can you imagine being stuck in a little house for so long?"

Feeling happy for Fred, Gary proudly announced, "I remember all the chess pieces now."

"This, we must check right away!" proclaimed Riddles as he took out a box of chess pieces.

"Great!" said Cassie, as she opened the notebook. "Once you answer all the questions we can continue our trip!"

HELP GARY ANSWER THE QUESTIONS
PUZZLES FROM THE NOTEBOOK

1. Point out the pawns, pal. How many black and how many white pawns are there?

2. Notice the noble knights. How many black and how many white knights are there?

3. Bring out the bishops, buddy. How many black and how many white bishops are there?

4. Root out the rooks from the rabble. How many black and how many white rooks are there?

5. Your question? Which are the queens? How many black and how many white queens are there?

6. Catch the kings by their crowns. How many black and how many white kings are there?

THE GATES OF CAISSIA

The three friends climbed aboard the six-seated tricycle and soon were again rapidly traveling through the countryside, with cities, forests and rivers rushing past in a blur of speed.

Finally, the travelers stopped before the walls of a magnificent city.

"Here it is. Caissia, the capital of our country!" Riddles said proudly. "It was named after Caissa, the Goddess of Chess."

"Look!" Gary exclaimed. "The city gates are in the shape of a chessboard!"

"Yes, and it is a very special chessboard," Cassie said. "Keep watching – in a minute, the chess pieces will set themselves in the starting position."

In a flash, four rooks appeared in the corners of the board, two white ones at the bottom, and two black ones at the top.

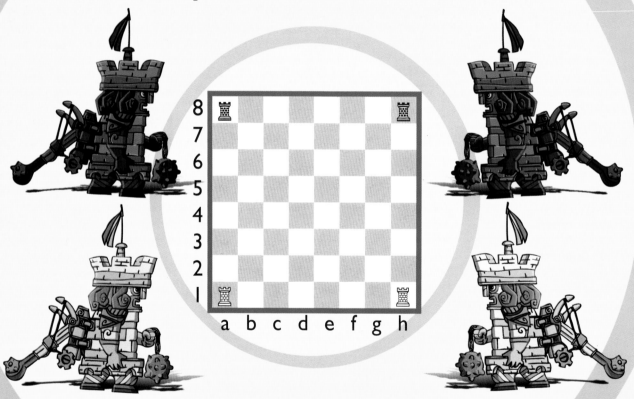

"The pieces are moving like in a cartoon!" Gary observed excitedly. "And the rooks are standing in the corners, like towers in a fortress."

"Remember, the white rooks start on the first rank, closest to the player who commands the white pieces," Riddles explained. "And the black rooks are on the last rank, next to the player who leads the black army."

Next to the rooks, on the first and last ranks, appeared the knights.

Then the bishops appeared next to the knights...

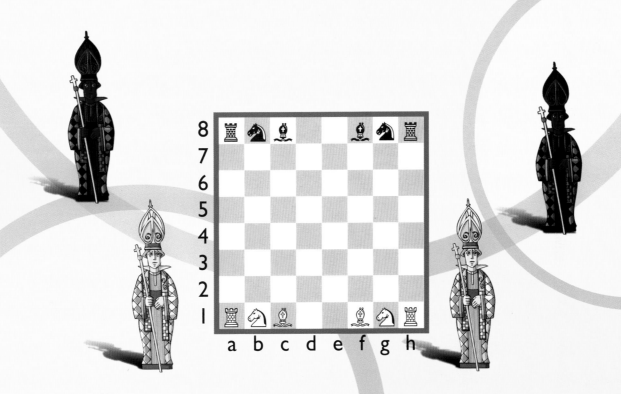

On the first and last ranks, there were only two empty squares now. As Gary looked on in amazement, the tallest chess pieces, the kings and the queens, took their positions in the centers of their armies. They bowed to the travelers, and Cassie continued.

"You need to remember where to put the queen and the king – don't mix them up," Cassie cautioned. "We have a great rule to help you remember what to do: The Queen Likes Its Color. It means that at the beginning, the white queen is on a light square, and the black queen on a dark square."

"What about the pawns?" Gary asked. "Do they start in the center?"

The pawns, as if they were waiting for this question, jumped on the gates one by one.

"The white pawns take up the whole second rank, and the black ones are right in front of the black pieces, on the seventh rank." Cassie answered.

Gary quickly counted the pawns.

"There are so many of them, as many as all the other pieces put together!" he said.

"Yes, exactly! Eight for each side," Cassie agreed. "At the beginning of the game, the pieces are set up this way. It's called the starting position."

Just then, Zug, the unfriendly boy, appeared in front of the gates.

"Still trying to learn? Good luck!" He snickered and kicked the gates. The white and black chess pieces scattered all over the road. A hidden door next to the gates burst open. By the time the guards came out, Zug had vanished. The guards saw the pieces lying on the road and gave Gary a stern look.

"It wasn't him! Gary would never do a thing like that!" Cassie said, trying to defend Gary.

Looking at her worried face, the guards softened. "We know you, Cassie and Riddles, and we trust you," their leader said, while still eyeing Gary with suspicion. "Why don't you just help us put the pieces back in their places?"

SET UP THE STARTING POSITION ON YOUR BOARD

"I remember," Gary said, "that the rooks are in the corners." And he carefully picked up the white pieces.

After the rooks, the knights, the bishops, and the other white pieces followed along. The guards brought a ladder, and Gary restored the black pieces to their positions at the top of the gates.

"Well done!" the guards said, smiling warmly at Gary. "Welcome to Caissia!"

"Let's go inside and do some puzzles," Riddles said.

HELP GARY SOLVE THE PUZZLES

1. Okay, now that you're so smart: set up the starting position on a board. How many white kings do you see? Queens? Rooks? Bishops? What about the black ones?

2. You can count on this – there are quite a lot of pawns. How many white pawns can you count? Black pawns?

3. If you ask them, they would never call themselves common, but which pieces are the most common on the chessboard? Which ones are the rarest?

4. They are not being punished, but which pieces start the game in the corners?

5. All right, we'll give you a clue: Cassie had a special rule for this one. What is the color of the square on which the black queen starts the game? Black king? White queen?

6. You should remember this one: on what ranks are the white pieces positioned?

7. How many pieces are on the first rank? Second rank?

8. How many black pieces are on the last rank? First rank?

9. A rook riddle: Show the files that have rooks on them. Bishops? Kings?

10. How many chess pieces are there on each rank?

11. Eight's a crowd: Are there ranks that have all their squares taken by pieces? How many ranks like that are there?

12. Can you find files (And not the computer kind!) that have pieces on all of their squares?

13. Remember Riddles' pointer: Show some diagonals that have chess pieces on them. Which ones have the most pieces?

14. Are there diagonals without chess pieces on them? Only one piece? Five pieces?

15. Monkey in the Middle! Are there any pieces in the center in the starting position?

23

Gary looked around this strange new city with great curiosity. The houses were shaped like chess pieces: huge rooks, magnificent queens, modest pawns. The people inhabiting the city looked cheerful and welcoming.

All except for Zug, who scowled at the group as they approached.

"Give up yet?" he snarled at Gary. "You might as well; here's where it gets tough."

The three friends shook their heads at the mean boy, who laughed and returned to his hiding place next to the gates.

"Among all the chess pieces, the rook follows the simplest rules of moving about the board," Cassie said as she directed the group towards the Rook's Place. "Today, we will take a closer look at what it can do and how."

"Why is the rook called the rook?" asked Gary.

Riddles jumped at the opportunity to show his knowledge.

"Very interesting question!" he said. "It probably came from the Persian word *rokh*, which meant 'chariot'. Chariots were ancient battle units, heavily armored to protect the driver and the archer inside. They did look like a moving tower!"

The travelers entered the palace and stopped before the door with a sign that read: "Rook's Place".

"Don't be too surprised by anything you see in here," whispered Cassie to Gary as she flung the door open.

After what he'd seen so far on this magical journey, Gary thought nothing could surprise him. He was wrong.

In the middle of the room, behind a desk in the form of a chessboard was sitting ... a Rook. A real rook, but live and smiling!

"Aha! Cassie and Riddles, nice to see you again!" said the Rook.

The handsome, powerful Rook looked Gary up and down. "And I see you brought a friend. Hello, young man," he addressed Gary. "As you have noticed, I am a Rook – I can teach you how we rooks move about on the chessboard. But first: when playing chess, the opponents take turns making moves. During each turn, you can only move one of your pieces."

The Rook added mysteriously, "There is, of course, an unusual double move, but we will talk about that later."

"Anyway, at the start of the game, White always moves first. Each chess piece has its own rules of moving about the board. We rooks can only move straight on ranks and files. In one move, a rook can skip any number of squares on a rank or a file as long as there is nothing in its way. Show him, little white rook!"

From the big Rook's belly, like out of a nesting doll, a small, white rook jumped out and skipped carefully from square to square, making sure to move only in straight lines, along the ranks and files.

The bigger Rook continued his lesson. "We can reach any square on the board. On an empty board, a rook can get anywhere in just two moves."

"But if there are other pieces in the way, whether our own or the opponent's, we can't jump over them or share the square with them."

Suddenly he looked up at Gary. "Are you paying attention, young man?"

Gary stared back, wide-eyed, nodding.

"As I was saying," the Rook continued, "we can't jump over pieces or share a square with them, but we can capture an opponent's piece that gets in the way."

"Capture?" Gary was surprised at all the new things he was being asked to learn.

"Capture, or take, means that the opponent's piece gets removed from the board and isn't allowed to play in the game anymore," Rook explained. "The rook that makes the capture takes over the square of the piece it captures. It all happens in one move."

The big Rook glanced at Gary. "Are you getting all this?"

Gary nodded quickly, anxious to hear the rest of the lesson.

"But here it gets harder," Rook said. "Unlike checkers, you don't have to capture your opponent's piece. To take or not to take, that is often the question in chess."

Just then, a little black rook jumped out of the big white Rook, climbed onto the board and prepared to demonstrate.

"Look, the black rook is under attack," Rook explained. "If it's White's move, I can land on it and take it off the board."

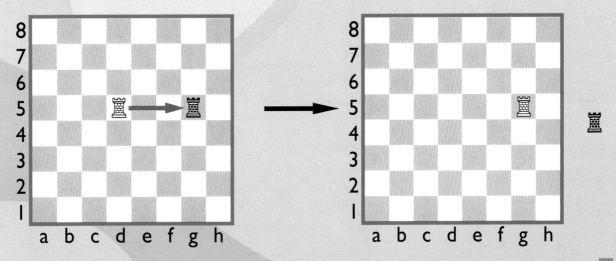

With that, the smaller white rook let out a squeak of delight as he captured the little black rook.

"And if it's Black's turn, I can capture the white one," added the little black rook. This time, he went over and, laughing in triumph, captured the white rook.

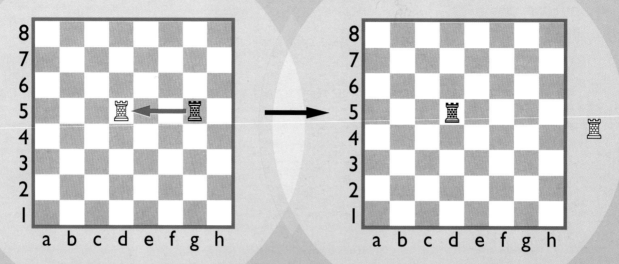

"This is all about the rules," the big white Rook continued. "Now you need to master them."

Gary correctly guessed that he was about to be tested again.

"Let's see if you can answer a few questions," the big Rook said with a smile. "First, how many moves does it take for a rook to get from one corner of the board to the opposite corner? Show me how to do it."

Answer the White Rook's Question

"It takes two moves," Gary said as he took the little white rook and moved it first to the end of the file, vertically, and then to the end of the rank, horizontally.

"Is that the only way?" Riddles asked.

Smiling, Gary shook his head as he reached over and moved the rook back, this time to the end of the rank first, then the file.

"Correct," Riddles said. "You're a fast learner. Question Two: How can a rook, starting from a corner, pass all the squares of the board, visiting each of them only once?"

HELP GARY

With Cassie's help Gary managed to solve the problem.

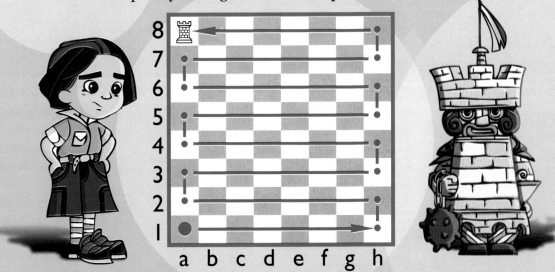

"Very good," the big Rook said. "By the way, there is more than one way of doing it, but your solution works just fine. Now, are you ready for a *real* challenge?"

Gary nodded excitedly.

"This next puzzle is called 'Outsmart the Guards'," the big white Rook told Gary, as he placed two black rooks and six white pawns on the board.

"The guards are the black rooks, and the white rook must outsmart them," Rook explained to Gary. "The white rook – think of it as a spy – needs to reach the opposite corner of the board."

Again, Gary nodded, never taking his eyes off of the board.

"It can only stop in the safe places - the squares where the black rooks can't capture it," the big Rook continued. "How many moves would it take?"

Gary was quite puzzled by the problem. At first, nothing worked. Every time the white rook tried to get closer to the target, a black rook would capture it, and Gary would have to start all over again.

Finally, he found the solution, and the little white rook, having passed the brigade of white pawns, safely arrived at the opposite corner.

"In four moves the spy can get through," Gary said.

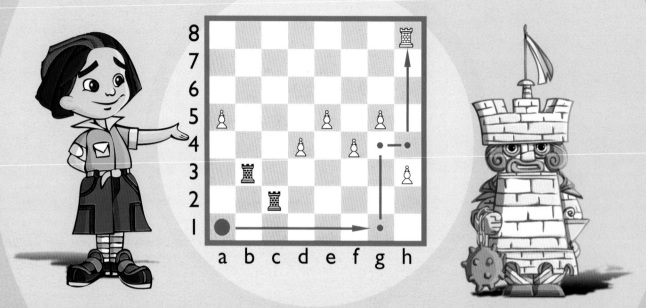

"Good job," the big white Rook said. "Here is a present for you, my little friend."

With that he handed Gary one of the small white rooks.

"I will be of service to you soon," squeaked the little white rook as it climbed into Gary's pocket.

"Let's solve some Puzzles from the Notebook and then run to the bishops. They are waiting," Riddles said, hurrying Gary along.

1. Don't be a square – you know the answer to this one. The rooks can move on which color squares?

2. He won't need a flashlight, but can a rook move from a light square to a dark square? From dark to light? From light to light? From dark to dark?

3. Maybe he's got the moves on the dance floor, but how many different moves can a rook standing in a corner make on the same rank? On the same file?

4. Muddle in the middle. How many different moves can a rook standing in a central square make on the same rank? On the same file?

5. All right, if you're so smart, how many different diagonal moves can a rook make from a corner? From a central square? Can a rook move diagonally?

6. Maybe a cow can jump over the moon, but can a white rook jump over a black rook? What about jumping over another white rook?

7. Here's a puzzle for you: set up the starting position on the chessboard. Can either of the rooks move?

8. He'll have to lace up his sneakers first, but how many moves will it take for a rook to run around the entire board stopping only in the corners?

9. Show a rook path that looks like a square. What about a rectangle?

10. Put on your thinking cap for this one. Put 2 (3, 4, 5, 6, 7, 8) rooks on the chessboard so that no two are on the same rank or file.

11. "Staircase" How can the rook in this diagram get to the opposite corner?   ⟶

12. 'To take or not to take?" Is it good for white to capture a black rook in these positions? (White doesn't want to end up losing his only piece!)

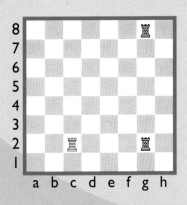

13. "Army of One" Capture all the black pieces with the white rook, taking one piece each move. (Only the white rook can move, the black pieces are "frozen".)

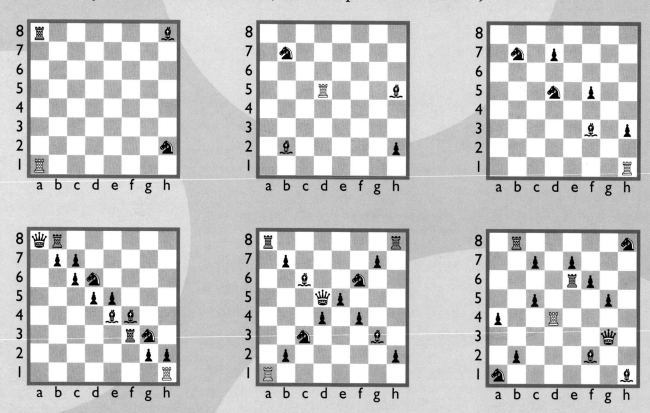

14. "Capture the Flag" What's the shortest path for White to capture the flag in these positions? (The rook cannot get on or slide over the mines.)

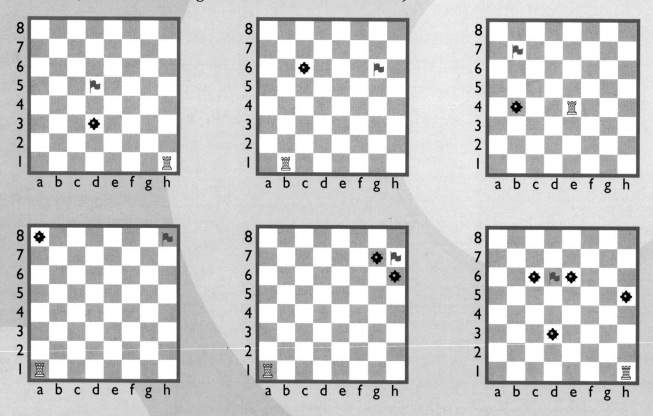

30

15. "The Amazing Maze" Get the rook to the square marked with a red flag without getting on or sliding over the mines.

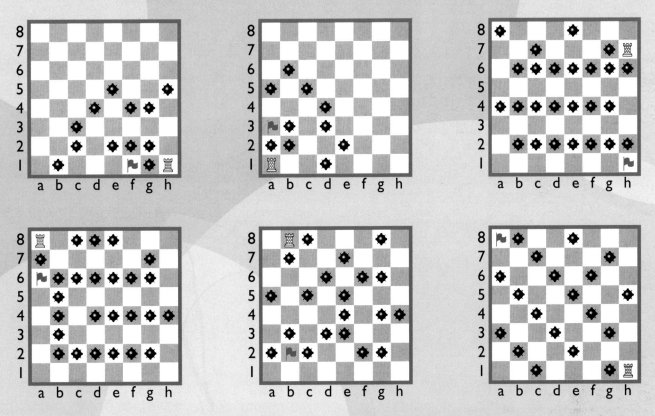

16. "Outsmart the Guards" With the white rook, sneak up to the square marked with a red flag without being attacked by the black pieces or triggering the mines.

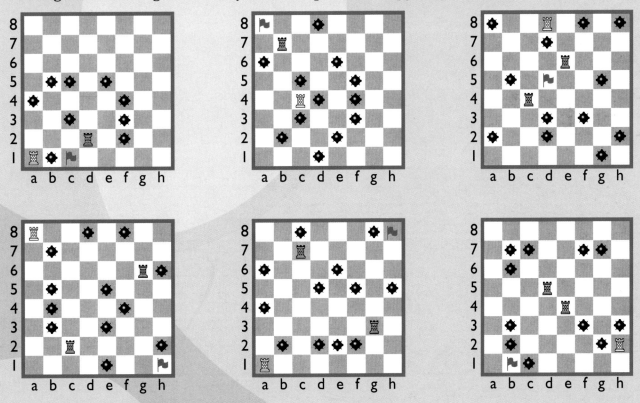

17. "Defend Home Base" Move the white rook so that Black can't move his rook to the marked square. (You cannot place your rook under attack.)

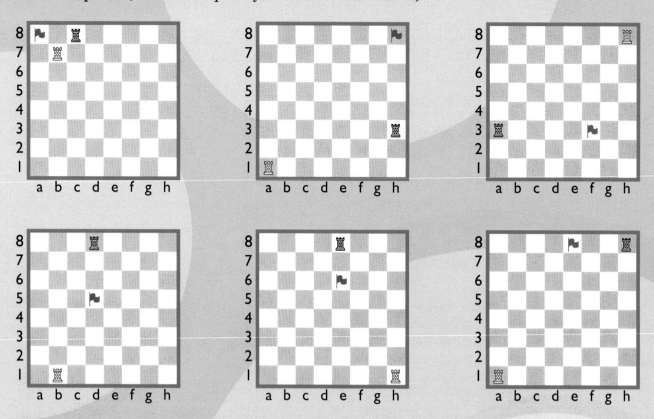

18. "Tied up in Knots" Figure out how the white rook can defeat the black one by forcing it to be under attack. (White and Black take turns to make moves.)

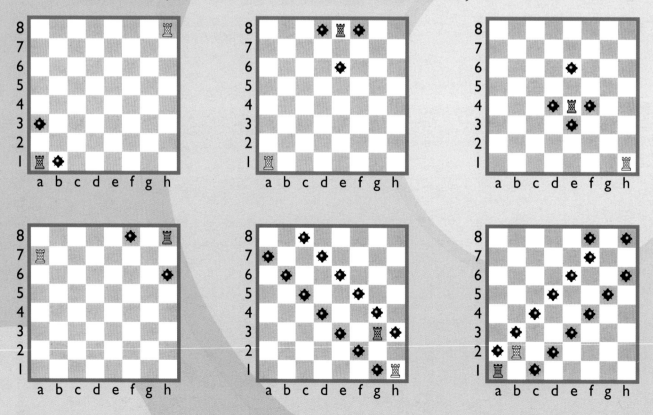

Chapter 7

The friends continued on their journey through Chess Country. Gary marveled at the amazing stores, restaurants, and movie theaters all shaped like chess pieces. Soon the trio stopped in front of a door that had two pointy-headed chess pieces pictured on it. Gary thought back to his previous lesson, and recognized the two as bishops. The friendly looking pair smiled as if inviting Gary and his pals to come in. Inside, there were pictures of elephants everywhere, and even the furniture and decorations were made to look like elephant tusks. Riddles, maybe thinking that Gary was confused, tried to explain.

"A long time ago, this piece, the bishop, looked like an elephant," he said. "The grooves you see were an elephant's tusks."

Gary squinted at Riddles, unsure if his friend was playing a trick on him. The sincere look on Riddles' face told him he wasn't.

"You see, the piece that we call 'bishop' has a lot of different names in other countries," Riddles continued. "The French call it the Fool. The Italians, Spanish and Russians call it the Elephant, and the Germans call it the Runner. And in English, 'bishop' is another word for a very important priest."

"Even the groove means different things to different countries," Riddles told Gary.

"It means 'fool's cap' in France, and 'headdress' in German," he said.

Just then the friends noticed two large bishops approaching them from different sides. One was white, and one was black. The first bishop introduced himself. "I am Whitesquare."

"Blacksquare," nodded the other, and after showing Gary and his friends where to sit down, he started the lesson.

"Bishops travel on diagonals; they can move one square at a time or a whole bunch," Whitesquare said. "Let me show you. Hey, little bishops, where are you?"

By now, Gary felt that nothing could surprise him. So when two small pieces, white and black bishops, approached the table, each hopping on one foot, then climbed up, he just grinned and waved in greeting.

The white bishop climbed up on the board and started running around, careful to step only on the dark squares.

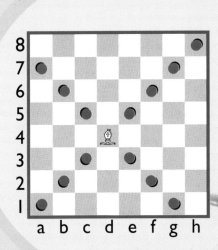

"Bishops, just like rooks, don't jump over other pieces," Blacksquare explained. "But, just like rooks, if on our way we encounter one of our opponent's pieces, we can capture it and take over their place. Like this!"

As Blacksquare said this, the little black bishop climbed up on the chessboard. No sooner had he settled on a dark square, the little white bishop captured him.

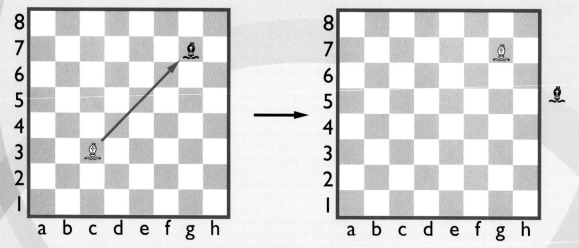

Gary stared at the board, thinking hard.

"If Black were to move first, then the black bishop would capture the white one, right?" he questioned.

"Very good," Whitesquare said happily. "You are a quick study. Now, let's see what else you've learned."

"Why are we called Whitesquare and Blacksquare?" the black Bishop asked.

Gary frowned in concentration. In his mind, he pictured the chessboard in its starting position. Let's see, he thought, concentrating on the board in his mind's eye.

"I've got it!" Gary said proudly. "In the beginning position, each player has two bishops – one on a light square and the other on a dark square. So, the bishop that goes only on light squares is a light-square bishop. The one that walks on dark squares must be the dark-square bishop, right?

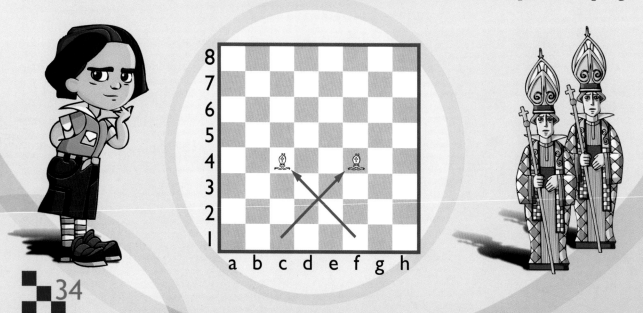

"Very good!" Riddles exclaimed. "I'm so pleased at how quickly you're learning the lessons."

"If during the game, the players end up with only one bishop each, and those bishops go on squares of different colors, they are opposite-colored bishops," Whitesquare said.

"But," added Blacksquare, "if they go on the squares of the same color, they are called same-colored bishops."

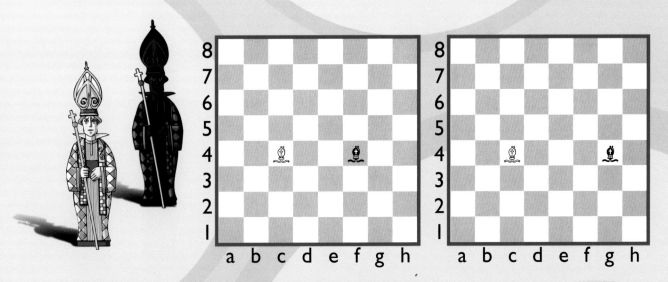

"What is stronger, a bishop or a rook?" Gary asked.

Riddles smiled that mysterious smile, and Gary sighed, knowing he was supposed to figure it out for himself. With his finger, he traced the files, ranks and diagonals again and again, frowning in concentration. How was he supposed to know?

Suddenly, his face brightened. "You guys can move both backward and forwards in two different directions," he told the bishops. "But in a rook's travels, he eventually can land on any square on the board."

Both bishops nodded encouragingly.

"Bishops can only move diagonally; you can't land on a different colored square than the one on which you started," Gary continued. "So really, you each only use half of the board. The rooks are twice as strong as you are!"

Cassie and Riddles beamed with pride, and both bishops clapped their hands as Gary blushed slightly at all the attention.

"But, we are more powerful in the center. We don't like being stuck in the corner," Whitesquare said.

"Neither do I," admitted Gary, ducking his head as he remembered how it felt to be stuck in a corner himself.

"From a corner, a bishop can attack fewer squares than from the center," Blacksquare explained. "Now, it's time for more puzzles. Let's put a bishop on the leftmost square of the first rank.

Can this bishop eventually reach every square on the board?"

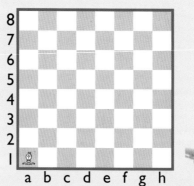

ANSWER BLACKSQUARE'S QUESTION

"No, not every square," Gary answered immediately. "It will NEVER reach a single light square!"

"Bravo!" Whitesquare cheered.

"One last puzzle from us. It's called, 'Outsmart the Guard.'"

Gary smiled; these were quickly becoming his favorite of all the puzzles.

"The light-square bishop has to sneak through to the opposite corner of the board without getting captured by the black bishop. How many moves will it take him to reach his goal?"

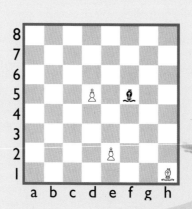

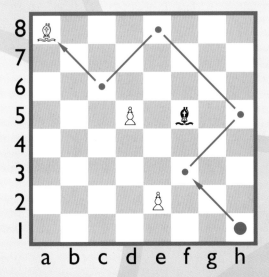

"In five moves," Gary announced confidently as he showed his solution to everyone.

"Brilliant! Good job!" both bishops said. "Here is a parting present to you from us, a little light-square bishop. Take good care of it."

"You will need me pretty soon," squeaked the little light-square bishop.

Gary gently picked up the little bishop, carefully placing it in his pocket, and said to Riddles, "I think it's time for me to do some more puzzles from your notebook."

HELP GARY SOLVE ALL THE PUZZLES

PUZZLES FROM THE NOTEBOOK

1. Even if you're colorblind, you shouldn't have any problem with this question: bishops move on which color squares?

2. He can stretch all he wants to, but what squares can't a light-square bishop reach? How about a dark-square bishop?

3. It's not really like hopscotch, but can a bishop move from one light square to another? From one dark square to another?

4. Don't let this question lead you in the dark. Can a bishop move from a dark square to a light square? From a light square to a dark square?

5. Even if he's wearing an awesome pair of sneakers, can a light-square bishop jump over a dark-square bishop? Over any white piece?

6. Don't let Riddles "get" you with this one: Can a light-square bishop capture a white rook? Can a light-square bishop capture a dark-square one?

7. Can a white bishop capture a black bishop? A black rook?

8. Think hard: Is it a good idea to give up your bishop, but capture one of your opponent's rooks?

9. Think harder: Can a rook always attack the opponent's bishop on a chessboard with no other pieces between the two?

10. Can a bishop always attack the opponent's rook on a chessboard with no other pieces between the two?

11. You remember how to do this first part. Set up the starting position. Can any of the bishops move? Why or why not?

12. Stand by me! In the starting position, what kind of bishop is next to the white king? White queen? Black king? Black queen?

13. You don't need a map to answer this question. In how many directions can a bishop go from a corner? From one of the central squares?

14. Get out of my way! Set 4 and 8 bishops on the board such that no two are located on the same diagonal.

15. 'To take or not to take?" Is it good for White to capture a black piece in these positions? (White doesn't want to end up losing his only piece!)

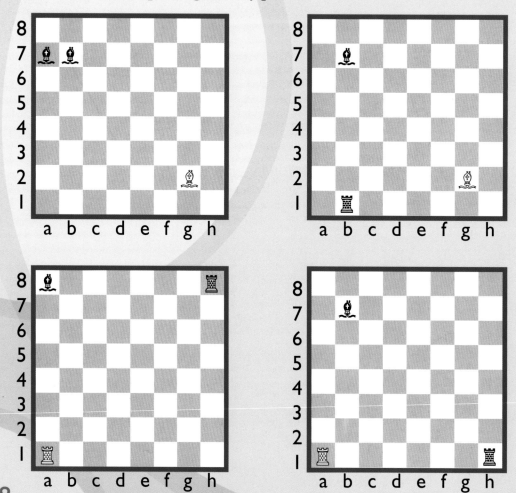

16. "Army of One" Capture all the black pieces with the white rook, taking one piece each move. (Only the white rook can move, the black pieces are "frozen".)

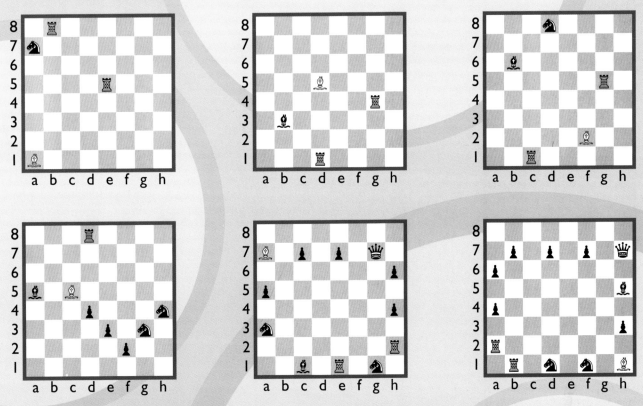

17. "Capture the Flag" What's the shortest path for White to capture the flag in these positions?

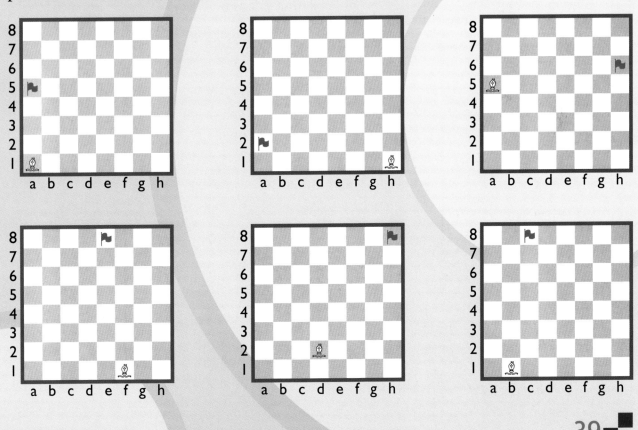

39

18. "Amazing Maze" Get the bishop to the square marked with a red flag without getting on or jumping over the mines.

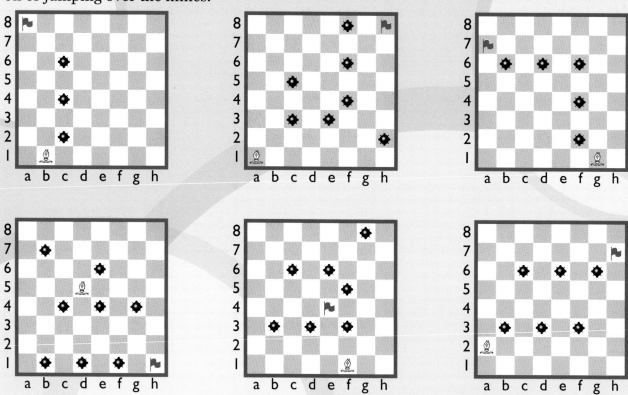

19. "Attack the Enemy" Attack the black bishop with the white rook (two ways) or the black rook with the white bishop.

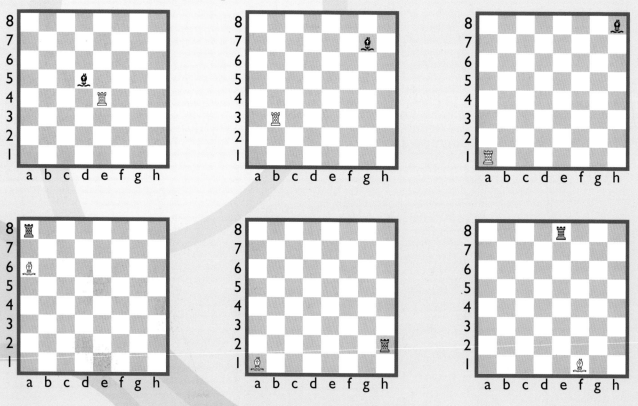

20. "Double Attack" Attack two black pieces with the white piece.

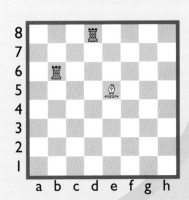
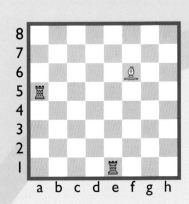
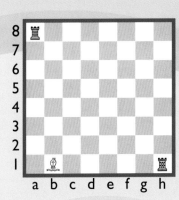

21. Capture the only black piece that is not protected by other black pieces.

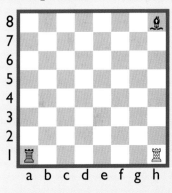

22. "Defense" How should White defend his bishop?

23. "Win a Piece" What move can White make now so he/she will win a black piece next move?

24. "Outsmart the Guards" With the white piece, sneak up to the square marked with a red flag without being attacked by the black pieces or triggering the mines.

 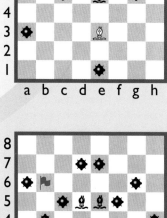 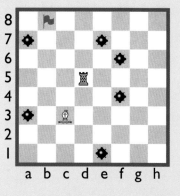

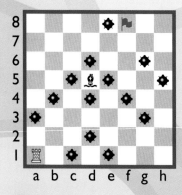 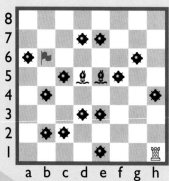 

25. "Stealth Fighter" With the white piece, capture the black pieces without being under attack ("stay off the radar screen") or stepping on the mines.

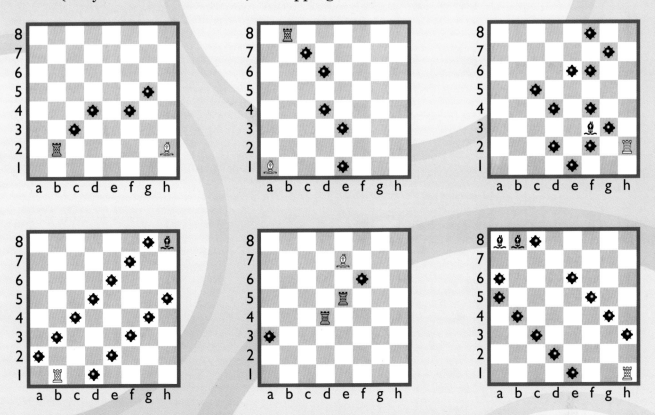

26. "Defend Home Base" Move the white bishop so that Black can't move her bishop to the marked square. (You cannot place your bishop under attack.)

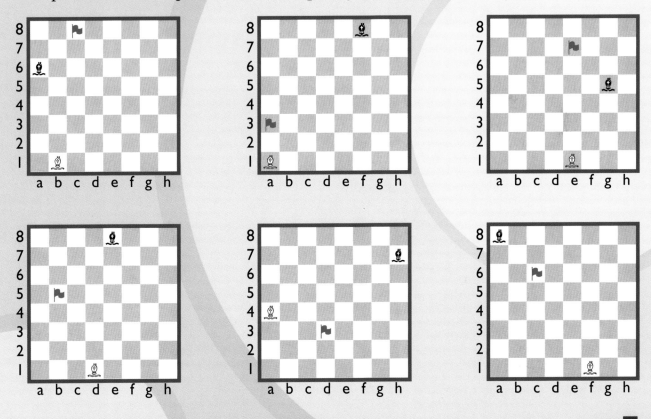

27. "Get to the Base" How can White reach the marked square in two moves? (White and Black take turns to make moves.)

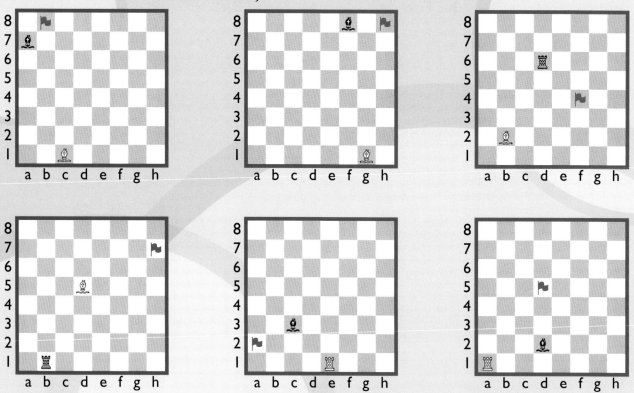

28. "Tied up in Knots" Figure how the white piece can capture the black piece by forcing it to be under attack. (White and Black take turns to make moves.)

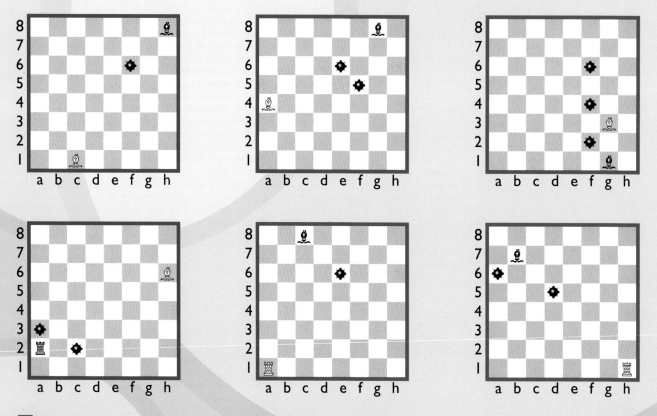

Soon the group was once again whizzing along the streets of Caissia on the tricycle. Gary's tiny new bishop friend squeaked excitedly in his pocket. As they came up over a hill, Cassie groaned in dismay and brought the tricycle to a sudden halt. Up ahead, Fred was running amok on the deserted street, trying to get away from Zug.

"I'm going to get you!" Zug panted as he chased Fred. "How dare you say that dumb kid can beat me at chess?"

Zug finally caught up with Fred next to the door to a hotel and tried to grab him. Fred easily dodged him and began running again. Gary jumped off the tricycle, yelling, "You leave my friend alone!"

"You-u?" Zug stopped in his tracks, blinking his eyes in confusion. "What are you still doing here? Haven't you given up yet?"

Seeing Cassie and Riddles standing right behind Gary, Zug must have known that he was outnumbered. He sneered at Gary one more time, before turning and walking away.

"Soon, my time will come," he said over his shoulder with a scowl. "Soon we will face each other across a chessboard, and then I will show you just how much better I am than you."

Gary watched him go, shaking his head in pity. "Why is he always so mean and angry?" he asked.

"Forget him," Cassie said impatiently. "We still have lots to do and places to go."

Fred smiled gratefully at his old friend. "Thank you, Gary. Thanks and... so long. Listen to your little friends."

"What little friends?" Gary was puzzled, but Fred had vanished from sight.

"Come on," Cassie said. "We're going to be late!"

"We don't want to keep the Queen waiting," Riddles cautioned.

Gary gasped as he caught sight of the majestic, powerful Queen. s

"The queen has been the strongest chess piece for the last 500 years," Cassie informed the group. "Before that, in the early version of the game, *shatranj*, there was a different piece in her place, called the vizier or the fers."

"Back then, the piece was a weakling, only able to move one square at a time," Cassie explained. It was hard for Gary to imagine such an imposing figure being weak or helpless. His disbelief must have shown on his face.

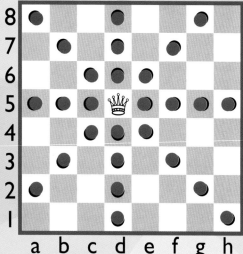

"Of course, the players need somebody with more power and skill," the Queen said haughtily. "Now, the queen can move like a bishop or like a rook. We move on ranks, files, or diagonals. No path is too long for us."

Right on cue, a small white queen appeared on the board and started running around, up, down, left, right and diagonally. Gary watched in wonder as the little queen touched every square on the board, moving in all sorts of directions.

"Like both the bishop and the rook, we cannot jump over other pieces," the Queen said, continuing her lesson. "But if there is an opponent's piece in our way, watch out! We can capture it and take its square."

A small black queen appeared on the board and the white queen captured it without hesitation.

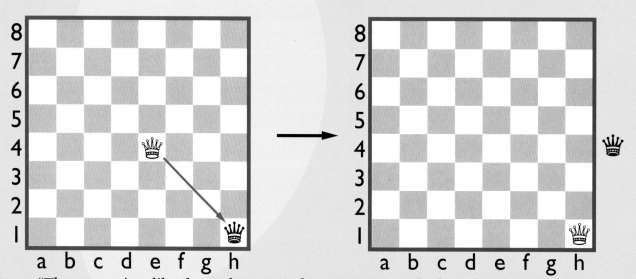

"The queen, just like the rook, can reach any square on the board in two moves," the big Queen said boastfully. "But tell me this, young man, how quickly can a queen get from one corner of the board to the opposite one?"

DO YOU KNOW THE ANSWER?

"The queen will go first by the file, then by the rank, like a rook. It can easily get across in two moves," Gary said.

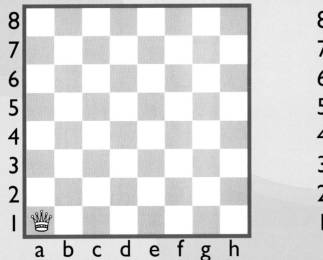
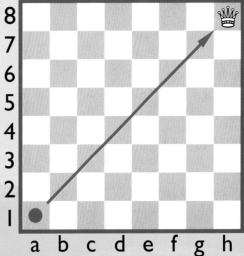

"Oh, no! Wait – even one move is enough for one as powerful as you. Because the queen can also move diagonally, like the bishop!"

"That's right, we can choose the way we move," said the big white Queen. "You are a smart boy. Now show me how a queen can visit all the squares of the board stopping at each of them only once."

HELP GARY

"Well," Gary said, carefully thinking of his answer, "the queen can move the same way a rook would."

"She can," added Riddles. "But she also can do something a rook can't," and he showed another route, like this:

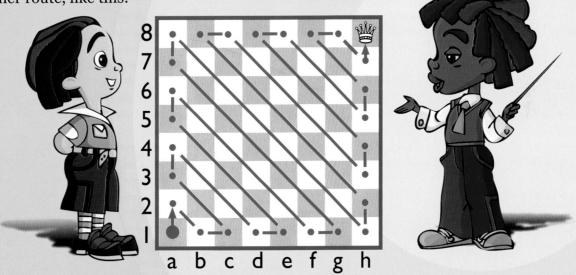

"Correct," agreed the queen. "We queens have our own special ways, but can also go the ways of the common folk."

"Here's one more task for you: outsmart the guard," Riddles said.

Gary smiled shyly, not wanting to look like a show off.

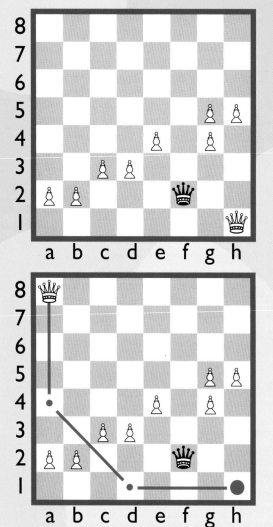

"The black queen is guarding the white one. The white queen wants to escape and get through to the opposite corner of the board. Can she do it? How many moves will it take?"

Though the black queen was a careful guard, Gary managed to find a way to get to the other side.

"Three moves and it's done!" he announced proudly. "Like this!"

"Very impressive, young man!" the Queen said as his friends clapped their hands in excitement.

The lesson was over and the big Queen gave Gary a present, a miniature version of herself. The tiny, squeaky-voiced queen happily joined her buddies in Gary's pocket.

"I must be off to do Queen stuff," the Queen informed her guests. "But you are welcome to stay the night, as it's getting late. Since you are such a good student you can even practice on my board if you like."

As his friends napped, Gary took out the notebook again and spent several more hours solving the problems.

When that proved too easy for him, he began making up some new problems for himself. This was so interesting that he couldn't stop. He was very tired, but stubbornly continued his exercises. The little queen, bishop, and rook squeakily advised, "It is late. Go to bed, or there might be trouble."

Gary was not taking the friendly suggestion.

"If you aren't interested in playing, just don't bother me, alright?" His voice sounded more irritated than he meant it to sound. He quickly added, "I'm sorry guys, why don't you just go to sleep." Then he put the pieces carefully into his pocket and zipped them inside.

Gary continued to work out chess puzzles, even as his eyelids grew heavier and heavier.

Finally, he nodded off to sleep, right over the chessboard.

Two hours later, somebody entered the room with a flashlight. A little cone of light centered on the notebook lying on the nightstand. The dark figure's nose cast a long shadow across the board.

"Finally, it is mine!" the night visitor cackled gleefully. "I will solve the problems and become the best chess player in Caissia. Look, here are some puzzles about the queen, let's try."

The sinister visitor peered in confusion at the pages. "I'm not sure what to do here... it must be too late at night. I'll try again tomorrow."

He scowled down at Gary, still fast asleep and now snoring lightly.

"And this guy? I'm going to lock him up for a week! He will forget everything he has learned so far."

Suddenly, Gary woke to the sound of his tiny friends, squeaking up a commotion. Blinking groggily, Gary peered at a strange and sinister-looking intruder. "What are you doing?" Gary asked. "What do you want?"

"I am here to take you to a secret place, to learn a chess move no one else knows," the stranger whispered mysteriously.

His voice sounded familiar to Gary, but in the dim light, he didn't recognize the shadowy figure. But of course he wanted to learn a chess move that no one else knew! He wanted to know everything!

Gary hesitated only for a second before following this odd newcomer.

Under his disguise, Zug was barely able to smother a laugh as he led Gary outside to his waiting buggy.

Solve the problems that Gary could do, but Zug couldn't.

PUZZLES FROM THE NOTEBOOK

1. Bet you a quarter that you know this about queens: On what squares do the queens move: the dark ones or the light ones?

2. She's packed her bags and she's ready to go! Can a queen move two squares over? Four squares over? Six squares over?

3. I know you can answer this quick question about the queen: Can a queen go from a light square to a dark one? From a dark one to another dark one?

4. Just how powerful is this queen? Can the white queen jump over a white rook? What about over black knight?

5. Set up the starting position. Can either queen move?

6. She won't need to look it up on the Internet, but in how many directions can a queen go from a corner? From a central square?

7. This chess piece has the moves, all right. How many different moves can a queen make along the same rank? What about a rook or a bishop?

8. How many different moves can a queen make along the same file? A rook? A bishop?

9. She didn't do anything wrong, but when she's standing in a corner, how many different moves can a queen make along the diagonal? What about a rook or a bishop?

10. Let's see just what that queen can do: can the white queen capture a black rook? A white rook?

11. Get ready for a challenge – set 2 queens on the board such that they are not attacking each other. Can you do four?

12. If you've been paying attention, you should know this one. Are there light-square queens? Black-square queens?

13. On a chessboard there are two pieces: black queen and white rook. Is it safe for the rook to attack the queen?

14. Is it always possible for the black queen to attack a white rook on a board free from other pieces? What about a light-square bishop instead of the rook?

15. Caution ahead: is it safe for the white queen to attack the black queen if there are no other pieces on the board?

16. Ladies and Gentlemen, start your engines! In the starting position, which queen (white or black) has a light-square bishop next to it?

17. 'To take or not to take?" Is it good for White to capture a black piece in these positions? (White doesn't want to end up losing his only piece!)

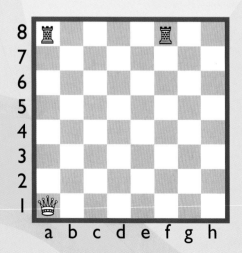
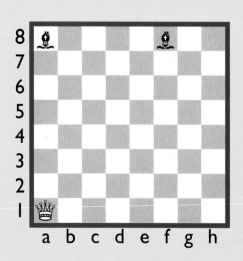

18. "Army of One" Capture all the black pieces with the white queen, taking one piece each move. (Only the white queen can move, the black pieces are "frozen".)

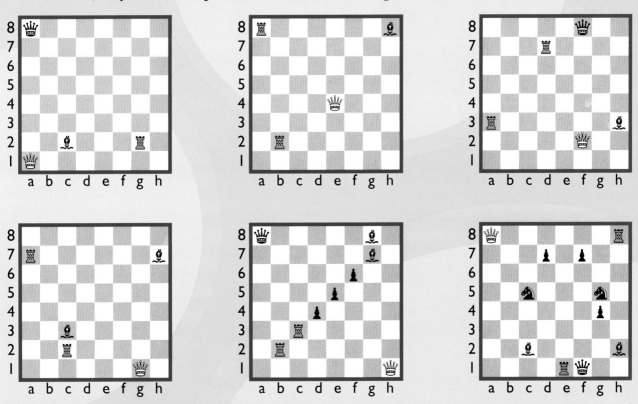

19. "Capture the Flag" What's the shortest path for White to capture the flag in these positions? (The queen cannot get on or jump over the mines.)

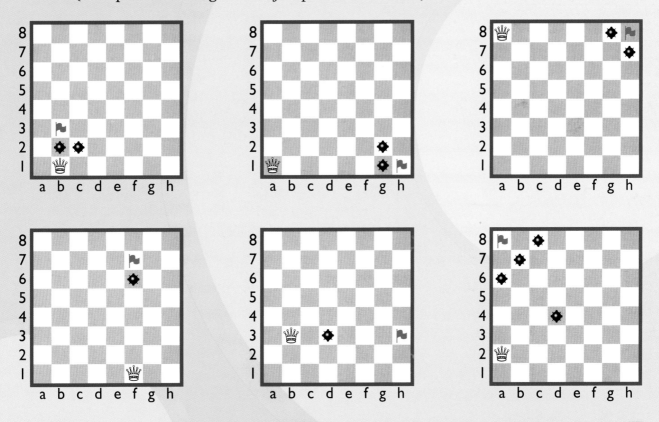

20. "Amazing Maze" Get the queen to the square marked with a red flag without landing on or jumping over the mines.

21. "Attack the Enemy" Attack the black bishop with the white queen (there are three ways to do this) or the black rook with the white queen (there is only one way to do this).

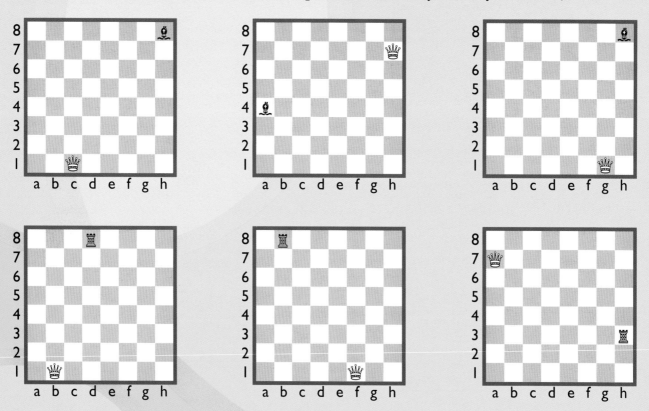

22. "Double Attack!" Attack two black pieces at the same time with the white queen.

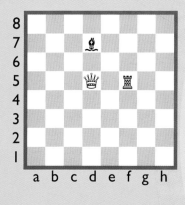  

23. Capture the only black piece that is not protected.

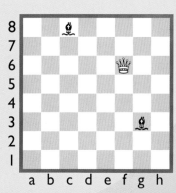  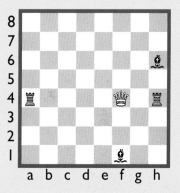

24. "Win a Piece" After which move can White capture a piece next?

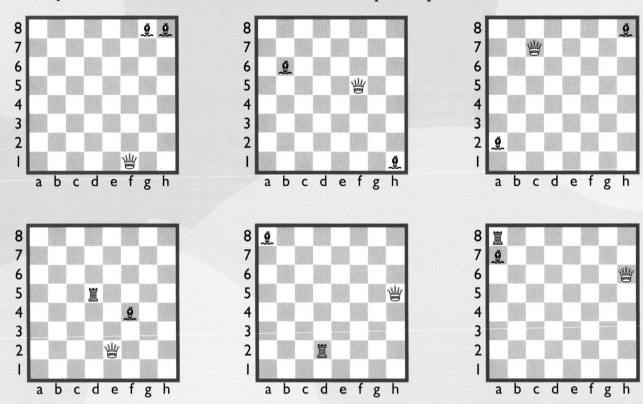

25. "Outsmart the Guards" With the white piece, sneak up to the square marked with a red flag without being attacked by the black pieces or triggering the mines.

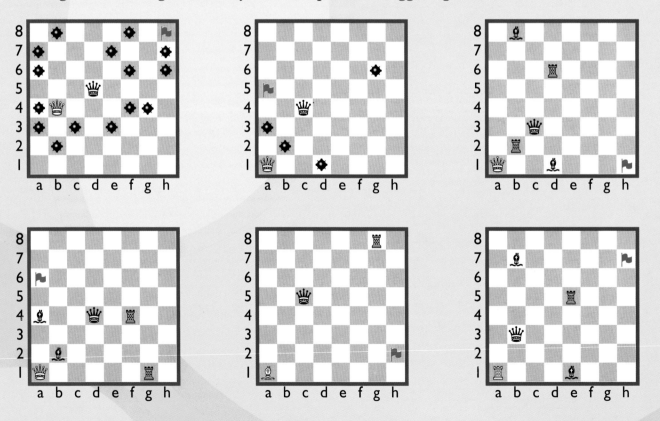

26. "Stealth Fighter" With the white queen, capture the black pieces without being attacked ("stay off the radar screen") or stepping on the mines.

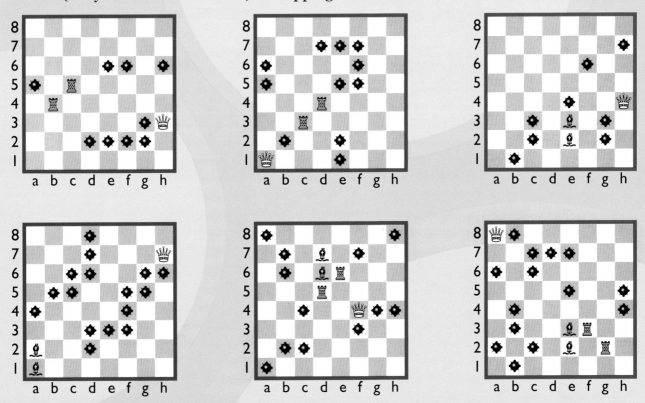

27. "Defend Home Base" Move the white queen so that black can't move his queen to the marked square. (You cannot place your queen under attack.)

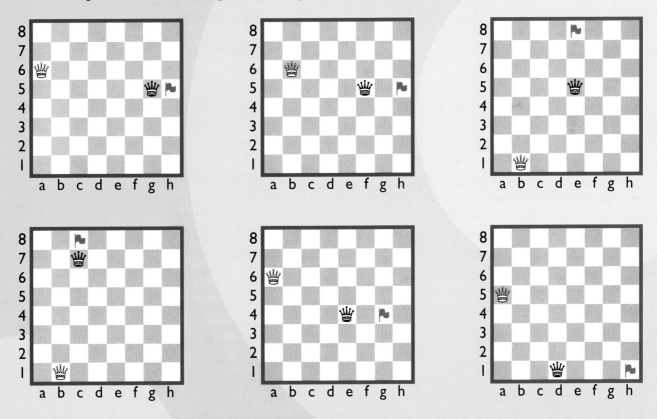

28. "Get to the Base" How can White reach the marked square in two moves? (White and Black take turns to make moves.)

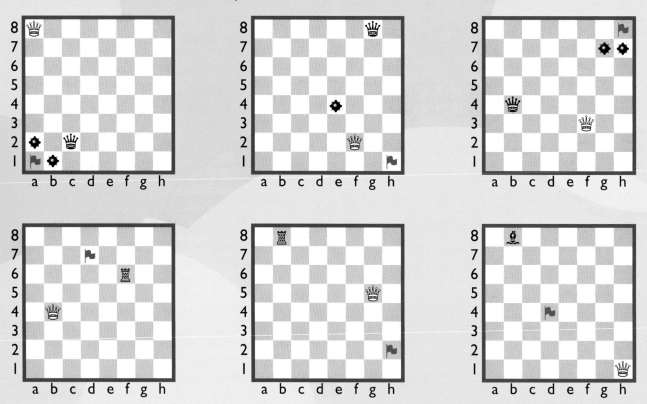

29. "Tied up in Knots" Figure out how the white piece can defeat the black piece by forcing it to be under attack. (White and Black take turns moving.)

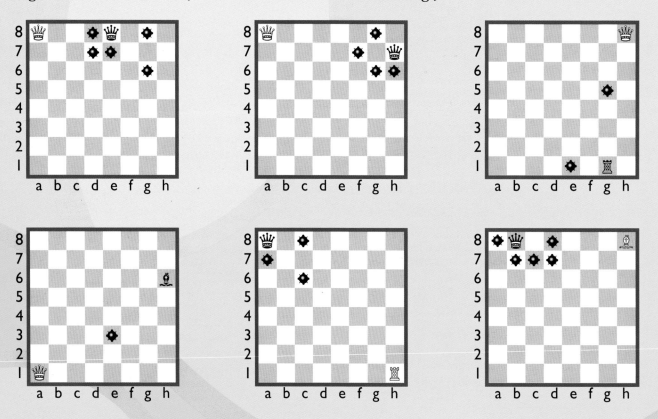

Gary was dreaming. In his dream, he saw Zug, who had turned into a horse. Zug was sneering even as he neighed.

"What's happening?" asked Gary in his dream.

"You will find out soon enough," Zug replied in a nasty tone.

Gary woke with a start. What was happening? He rubbed his eyes and blinked rapidly, trying to clear his fuzzy mind. Was he dreaming? Was he awake? What had just happened? He did hear a horse neighing. "I must be sleeping," he said to reassure himself. "I must be dreaming about my next lesson with the horse-mounted knights."

It was still dark. Gary tried to move, but he was completely tied up! This time he had no doubts he heard the real Zug saying, "After I lock the stupid boy in the closet, should I keep him there for a week or two? Nobody will find him there anyway!"

Gary realized he was in big trouble, and completely at Zug's mercy. Why hadn't he listened to his little friends, the chess pieces? And what was it that he was moving in?

It was Zug's buggy, speeding through the streets of Caissia, carrying Gary along. Oh, he was hoping that something interesting would happen to him, but this was much too interesting.

Suddenly, Gary heard the familiar, "Ring-ding-ding!"

Fred!

Indeed, Fred had caught up with the buggy. He was sitting next to Gary trying to cut the ropes with a sharp stone. It was not going well. Fred looked tired and frustrated.

Then a squeak came from Gary's pocket: "Please let us out!"

Fred unzipped the pocket and the tiny queen, rook, and bishop popped out. The pieces took turns helping Fred.

"Bishop, why don't you use your pointy head to cut through the rope!" Rook exclaimed.

It worked, and finally, the prisoner was free. They all jumped off to safety, and Gary thanked his friends. Then they watched as Zug and his buggy disappeared into the distance.

"Hello, little friend," a deep voice said right next to Gary.

He jumped and turned. Standing nearby was a knight sitting atop a magnificent horse.

"My friend, the chess knight," Fred said by way of introduction. "It was he who helped me catch up with the buggy and rescue you."

"You see," Fred continued, "even on the chessboard knights move in an unusual way."

"Will you tell me about it?" Gary asked eagerly.

"Of course! But first you probably need some rest and food. The knight will take us to the castle that he shares with his friends."

The knight lifted everyone up onto his saddle. The horse galloped away. After a while they reached the castle, and on its gates Gary saw a huge letter L painted as if sitting on a horse.

After breakfast, Gary was invited to the common room, where a horse greeted him.

"My knight is very busy again," the horse said. "Something to do with a big meeting with the king. So I will be showing you the moves."

Gary smiled. He knew horses were smart, but he'd never been taught by one before!

"In fact," the horse continued, "very often the knights are too busy to play chess, too. So we, the horses, do it ourselves. It's fun and we don't mind it, actually. That's why the chess piece 'knight' is often shown as if there were no knight on the horse!"

The horse took out the chessboard.

"At the starting position, there are four knights on the board – two black ones and two white ones. The chess knight is a very tricky piece! On the board we move like this: two squares up or down and then one square left or right. Or, the other way: first two squares left or right, and then one square up or down."

"That's why the knight move looks like the letter L!" Gary exclaimed.

"Very good," the horse said, smiling at Gary. "I heard you were a smart boy, and I see that what I heard was correct."

Just then, a little white horse jumped into the center of the board and showed all of the squares it could reach with a single move.

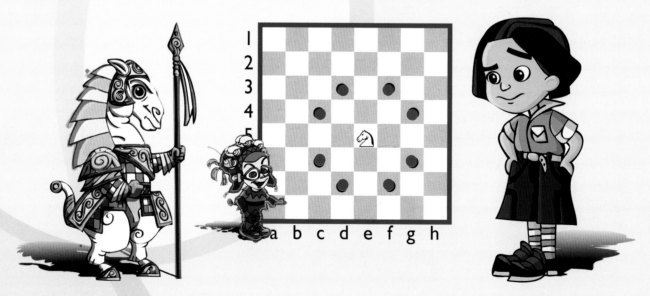

Gary watched carefully.

"So from the center you can reach eight different squares," he observed.

Gary kept watching as the knight moved into a corner. Then, the knight showed which squares it could reach in a single move.

"You can only reach two squares from the corner!" Gary said, proud of himself for counting correctly.

"Very good!" the horse praised him again. "That's why the chess pieces often say, 'Knight on the rim is grim!' Because if he's stuck on the edge of the board, there aren't too many places a knight can move."

Gary studied the board some more, as the little knight continued its L-shaped dance moves around the chessboard.

"You can reach any square, just like the rooks and queens," he said.

"Correct again," the horse said enthusiastically. "But we knights can do something no one else can! We can jump over other pieces, both our own and our opponent's. It's a special power! If a square that a knight is aiming for is already taken by an enemy's piece, we can capture it. But we don't take what we jump over."

The horse put a little white knight in the corner, and a little black knight nearby, like this:

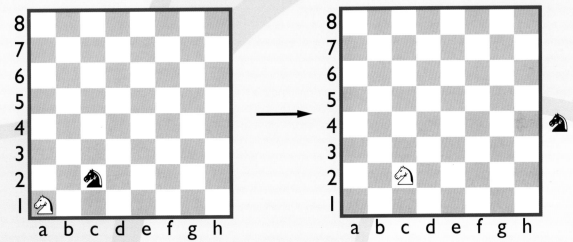

"This is how a white knight (on White's move, of course) can capture the black knight," the horse explained.

"But if it is Black's move," Gary said, "then the black knight can capture the white one."

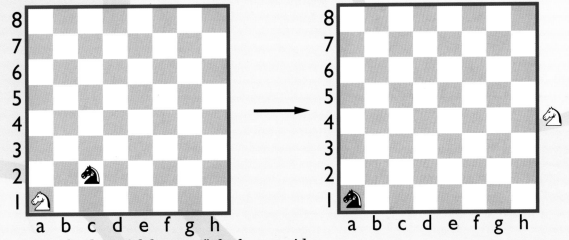

"You are indeed a quick learner!" the horse said.

Gary blushed at the praise.

"Are knights as strong as rooks, or as strong as bishops?" he asked.

"On the chessboard a knight has the same value as a bishop, but we're a bit weaker than a rook or a queen," the horse explained. "That's why the rooks and the queens are called the major pieces, and the bishop and the knight – minor pieces."

Gary thought hard over his previous lessons.

"So," he began slowly. "If you can capture an opponent's rook while giving up a bishop or a knight, then you come out ahead, right?"

"Exactly!" the horse said. "In fact, trading a bishop or knight for a rook is often called winning the exchange."

Gary smiled. It was all coming together in his mind, and this game of chess was starting to make sense.

"I think I'm ready for some puzzles now," he said confidently.

"Very well," the horse said with a smile. "Here is the first: How can the knight capture the black queen in two moves? Just remember that, for this puzzle only, the black queen can't move. Consider her frozen in place like a snowman. Or, I should say, a snow queen."

While Gary was thinking, Fred whispered something to the little white knight. The knight jumped once, twice, and the black queen was captured.

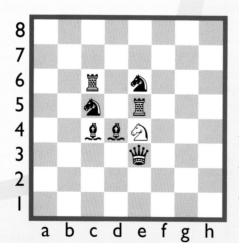

"Keep your two cents to yourself!" the horse, smiling, said as he wagged a hoof at Fred. "Now Gary will get a different puzzle. In this position on the board, how can the white knight capture all the black pieces, getting them one at a time?"

CAN YOU SOLVE THIS PROBLEM?

Gary studied the board for a moment, then figured out how to do it. The white knight rushed around the center of the board capturing the black pieces.

60

"Excellent!" the horse exclaimed.

The little Queen, Bishop and Rook peeked out of Gary's pocket and beckoned the little Knight to join them. And, of course, he did.

Gently patting his pocket to ensure that his little friends were secure, Gary wondered what Zug must have thought when he got home and found his buggy empty, his captive escaped.

With a jolt, Gary realized that in their haste to escape from Zug's clutches, they had forgotten Riddles' valuable notebook!

Meanwhile, Zug was in for a big surprise. "How could that have happened?" the boy exclaimed when he arrived home and realized Gary was no longer tied up in the back of the buggy.

He couldn't understand how Gary had escaped. "Well, at least I have the notebook," he grumbled, and opened it to the chapter that had the problems about the knights.

But no matter how he tried, Zug couldn't solve even half of the puzzles.

CAN YOU SOLVE THEM?

PUZZLES FROM THE NOTEBOOK

1. First, a few basic dance steps. On which squares do the knights move: the light ones or the dark ones?

2. Even though he's wearing armor, he still has the moves, but can a knight go from a dark square to a light one? From a light one to a dark one?

3. It's shaped like a horse, but can a knight jump over the other pieces?

4. Meet you in the Winner's Circle if you can do this one. Try to move a knight from the first rank to the last one. How many turns did it take? Can you do it faster?

5. It's a horse race! Move a knight from one corner of the board to the opposite corner. What's the fastest way to do it?

6. We can count on you to figure this one out: in how many moves can a knight get to the next (on the same rank) square? What about a next square on the same file?

7. Even though he's in a meeting, the big Knight knows that you can do this. How many moves does it take for a knight to get from a central square to the next square on the same diagonal?

8. This one's tough, so I hope you were paying attention: how many moves would it take for a knight to get from a corner to the next square on the same diagonal?

9. Is this too close for comfort? Can a knight capture an opponent's piece standing next to it?

10. In the starting position, can any of the knights make a move? If yes, how many different ones?

11. The battle has begun! From what position does a knight attack more squares, from the center or from a corner?

12. Step lightly! Can a light-square bishop attack a knight standing on a dark square?

13. "To take or not to take?" Is it good for White to capture a black piece in these positions? (White doesn't want to end up losing his only piece!)

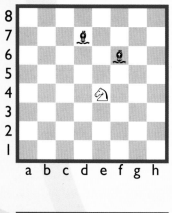
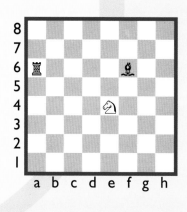

14. "Army of One" Capture all the black pieces with the white knight, taking one piece each move. (Only the white knight can move, the black pieces are "frozen".)

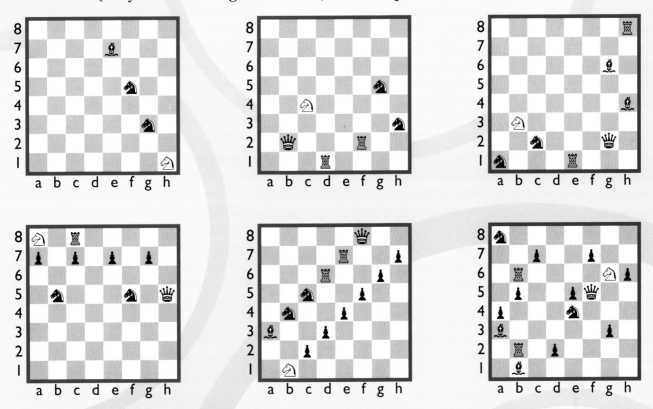

15. "Capture the Flag" What's the shortest path for the white knight to capture the flag in these positions?

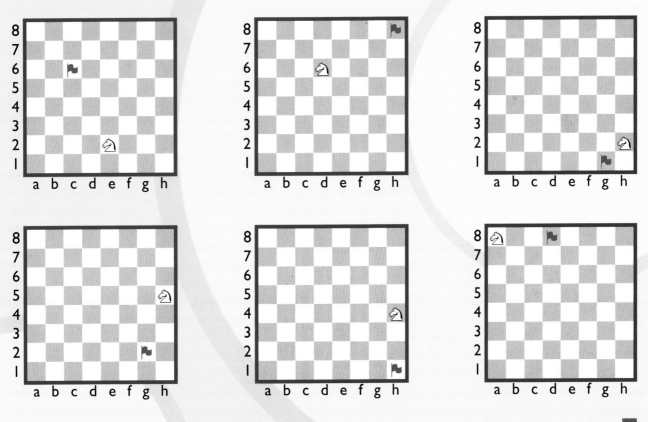

16. "Amazing Maze" Get the knight to the square marked with a red flag without landing on the mines.

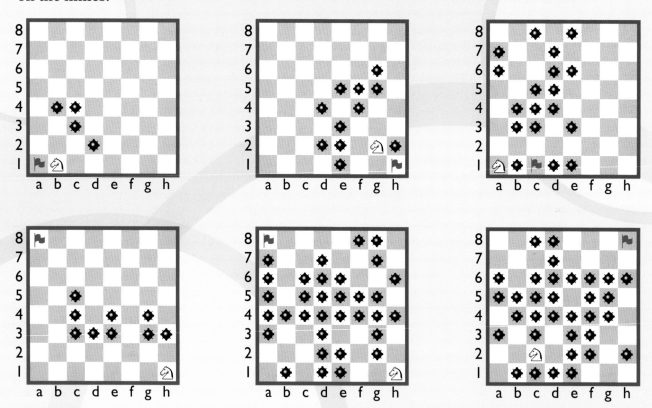

17. "Attack the Enemy" Attack the black piece with the white knight.

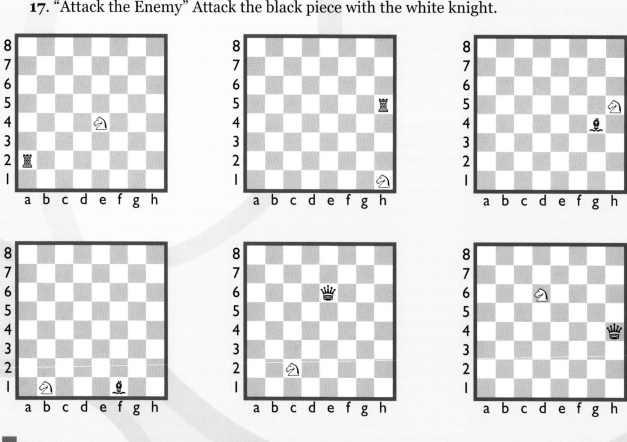

64

18. "Double Attack" Attack two black pieces with the white piece.

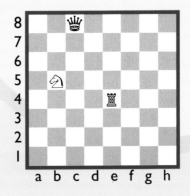
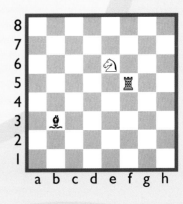

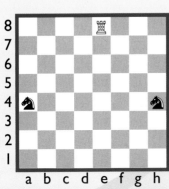
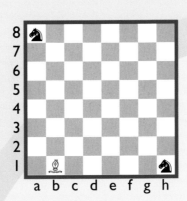

19. Capture the only black piece that is not protected.

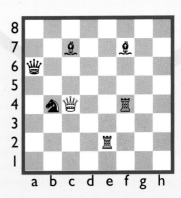

65

20. "Defense" What move should White make to avoid losing a piece?

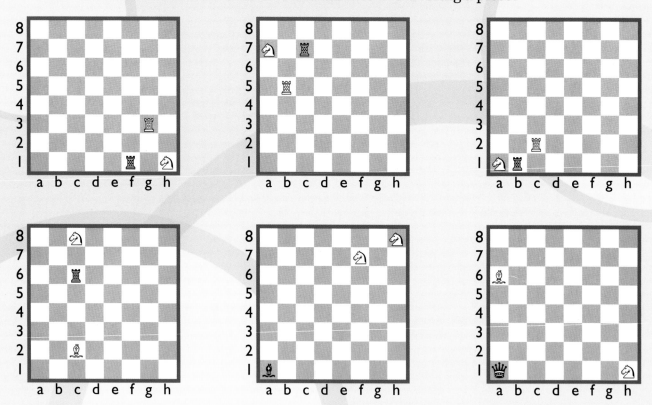

21. "Win a Piece" After which move can White capture a piece next?

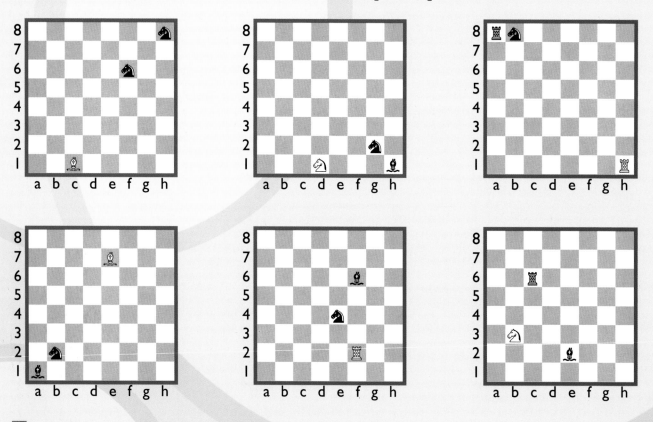

22. "Outsmart the Guards" With the white piece, sneak up on the square marked with a red flag without being attacked by the black pieces or triggering the mines.

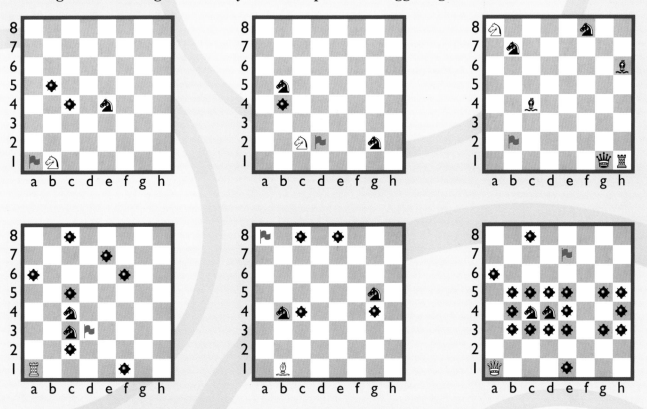

23. "Stealth Fighter" With the white piece, capture the black pieces without being under their attack ("stay off the radar screen") or stepping on the mines.

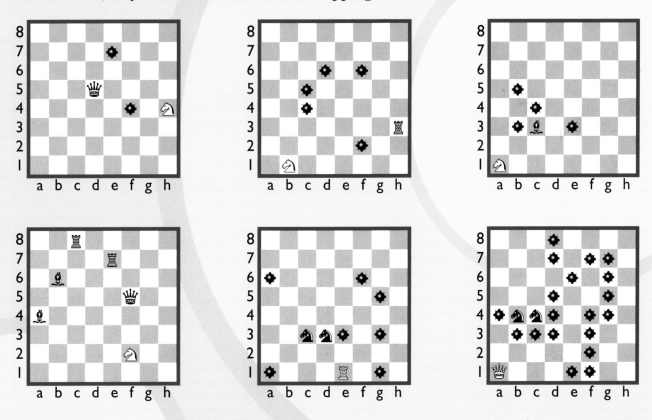

24. "Get to the Base" How can White reach the marked square in two moves? (White and Black take turns moving; Black is trying to prevent White from reaching White's goal without putting his own piece under attack.)

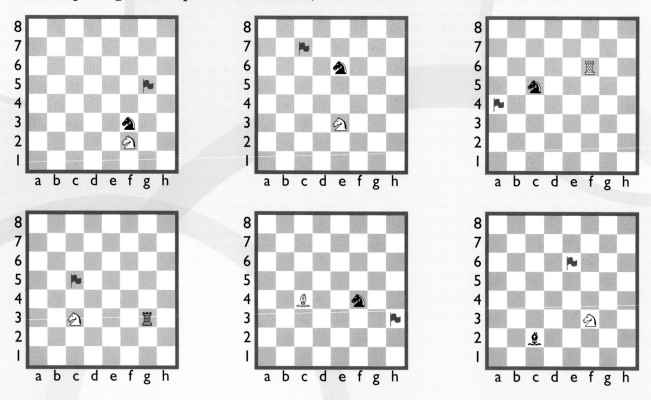

25. "Tied up in Knots" Figure out how the white piece can defeat the black piece by forcing it to be under attack. (White and Black take turns moving)

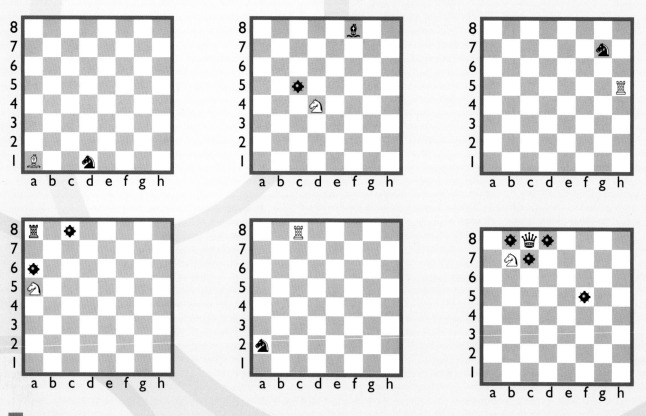

26. "Taming the Wild Horse" In the following diagrams white pieces are missing. (In the first diagram, the white rook is missing, in the second, it's the light-square bishop, in the third and the fourth, it's the white knight, and in the fifth and the sixth it's the white queen.) Put the missing pieces on the board so that wherever the black knight moves, it would get captured by White.

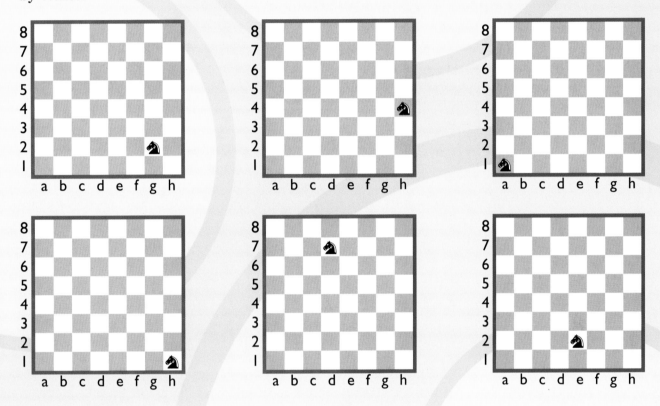

Gary, Cassie, and Riddles were full of despair – the precious notebook had disappeared! They had a feeling that Zug had stolen it, but what should they do now?

"OK," said Riddles with authority. "You cannot learn chess by sitting around and feeling glum. I remember the puzzles even without the notebook."

Gary's eyes widened. "All of them?"

"Ahhmmm, er, well, most of them." Riddles blushed. "Well, most of the knight ones. I…I think," he stammered.

"That's perfect!" Cassie jumped in. "Try to remember what puzzles you can. After that, you and I will go look for the notebook and Gary can move on to the pawn lesson."

Thinking over what the horse and his little knight friends had taught him, Gary easily finished the problems that Riddles recreated from his memory.

Soon they were speeding off to the next lesson. Gary felt excitement growing in his chest as he wondered whom, or what, he would meet next. Much to his surprise, the group soon came to a place called "Pawn Kindergarten."

"A kindergarten?" Gary said, scratching his head. "What can a bunch of little kids teach me about chess?"

"Why don't you go inside and find out?" Riddles suggested.

When Gary stepped inside, he saw the kindergarten children playing various games and coloring. Most of the kids seemed happy, except for one little freckled girl, who ran up to them as soon as she saw Gary and his friends.

"Alex called me weak," she said, starting to sob.

"What for?" Gary said. "What happened?"

"We were playing. I was pretending to be a bishop, and he was a rook. Then he said 'A rook is stronger than a bishop,' and he laughed at me."

"Don't pay any attention to him," Gary said. "First, bishops can, and have, captured rooks. Second, only small-minded people bully others. Next time someone tries to bully you, you just tell them that they think like a pawn, and you think like a queen."

The girl smiled gratefully and ran away to play with the others.

Then Gary saw a large group of kids huddled together around something. He came closer and saw a big white Pawn sitting at a table with little pawns surrounding him, like chicks gathered around a hen.

"Sit down, sit down, and make yourselves comfortable," the pawn said to Gary and his friends. "Do you remember the starting position?"

"Sure," Gary said instantly. "There are eight white pawns in the second rank and eight black pawns in the seventh rank."

"Bravo!" The big white pawn applauded. "Remember, pawns are small, but they are very brave. Like infantry, we never retreat, we always charge ahead, one square at a time along the file."

Just then, little white and black pawns took their starting positions on the board and took turns moving, some one square ahead, others two squares at a leap.

"Hey, what are you doing?" Gary exclaimed. "I thought pawns could only move one square at a time!"

"Ah, very observant," the big Pawn said with a smile. "We can go two squares ahead only from the starting position. But that's if there is nothing in the way, and if we've had a good, healthy breakfast in the morning for extra energy."

"But you can't jump other pieces, only knights can do that," Gary recalled from his previous lesson.

Gary was confused by this new move. He watched the little pawns on the board over and over as he tried to make sense of it.

"It looks as if the opponent's pawn moved only one square ahead and got captured there," the big white Pawn explained. "You cannot wait with capturing en passant; it is now or never. En passant is only possible for one move. Also, no other piece can capture or be captured en passant."

"We may be small, but we do have some abilities that no one else on the chessboard has!" boasted one of the small pawns standing near the table.

"It gets even better," added the big Pawn. "We don't always stay small the entire game. If a white pawn can reach the last rank (or the first rank for a black pawn), it can become any piece, except the king. Most of the time, we want to become the strongest piece, the queen. This magical transformation is called a promotion."

"I think it happens in real life, too." Gary said quickly. "I remember my mom saying she wanted to be promoted."

"Yes, and it happens in stories as well. Remember Cinderella? She married the Prince and was promoted to a queen also. Here's how it happens in the game of chess," the Pawn said as he pointed at the board.

A little white pawn moved one square ahead and reached the last rank. Then, it quickly jumped off the board. Jumping out of Gary's pocket, the little white queen hurried to take the pawn's place.

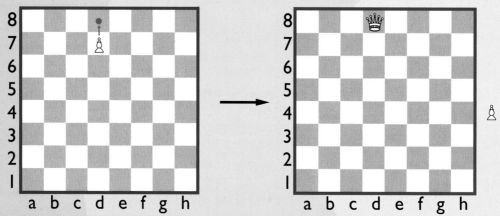

"Now, the questions," said the big white Pawn. "How many moves will it take for a white pawn to walk across an empty file and reach the last rank from the starting position?"

DO YOU KNOW THE ANSWER?

"Six," said the freckled girl.

"It can do it even faster, in five moves," Gary corrected. "Because the pawn can jump two squares ahead from the starting position."

"Right, Gary, very good!" the big Pawn said. "How about this one: can a pawn visit all the squares of the chessboard?"

WHAT DO YOU THINK?

"No!" all the other children replied in unison.

Gary smiled. He realized why it was such a tricky question. "Yes, it can. It can get to the last rank, turn into a queen, for example, and walk to any square it wants!"

"Perfect!" the big Pawn said, smiling again at Gary. "Now the last question: look at the board and tell me what moves the white pawn can make!"

SOLVE THIS PROBLEM TOO:

"The white pawn can capture either the rook or the queen," Gary said. "It can also move ahead to the last square of the file."

"And turn into any other piece on any of these three squares, except for the king, of course," the freckled girl quickly added, looking pleased to have caught on.

"Good job, everybody!" said the big white Pawn. "That was our entire lesson."

Once the big Pawn finished, the little white pawn hopped off the board and right into Gary's pocket. The little queen who had helped with today's lesson followed close behind. The pawn was definitely in good company.

Only when the lesson was over did Gary realize how much time he had spent at the kindergarten; it was completely dark outside. He went to rejoin Riddles and Cassie, and found them frustrated and worried. They had spent the entire day searching the city, but found no trace of Zug or the notebook.

"Tomorrow is a new day!" a familiar voice said, and Gary saw Fred joining them. "Why don't you guys get some rest, and I will see if I can help?"

When it got completely dark and the city fell asleep, Fred climbed up the tallest tower in

Caissia. From the tower he could see the only house, next to the palace, that still had its lights on. And he could see into the window.

It was Zug, trying to do the pawn problems! Do you think he solved them, without even hearing the lesson of the big white Pawn? Of course not!

CAN YOU SOLVE THE PUZZLES FROM THE NOTEBOOK?

1. Don't be a square, you know this one! On what squares move the pawns, dark or light?

2. Pawns aren't afraid of the dark. Can a pawn move from a dark square to a light one? From a light one to a dark one? From a dark one to another dark one?

3. Put the brakes on, buddy. Can a pawn move two squares ahead?

4. Lace up your sneakers! Can pawns jump over other pieces?

5. How does a pawn capture other pieces? (And don't say with a net!)

6. Answer this, without using a map: in how many different directions can a pawn capture?

7. It's getting crowded down here! Can there be two white pawns on the same file? What about three white pawns?

8. You might want to think this over for a minute: do pawns move the same way as they capture?

9. In the starting position, how many different moves can each pawn make?

10. Don't forget your lessons! How many rook pawns are there at the beginning? What about queen pawns or knight pawns?

11. Answer this without getting dizzy. Can a rook pawn capture in two different directions?

12. Can a knight pawn capture a bishop pawn?

13. Remember your French lessons: does a pawn have to capture en passant?

14. Can a pawn capture a rook en passant?

15. Pawns work really hard to get this: To what pieces can a pawn be promoted?

16. If a pawn works really, really hard, can it get promoted to a king?

17. Don't bump into the sofa! Do pawns move backwards? Do they capture backwards?

18. Gary figured this out, but do you know it? What rank does a black pawn need to reach to get promoted? What about a white pawn?

19. Can pawns move horizontally, along a rank?

20. Watch out buddy, I'm coming through! Can a pawn move ahead if the square in front of it is taken by another piece?

21. Getting greedy? Can a pawn capture two pieces in one move?

22. Can a white pawn get promoted to a black piece?

23. "To take or not to take?" Is it good for White to capture a black piece in these positions? (White doesn't want to end up losing her only pawn!)

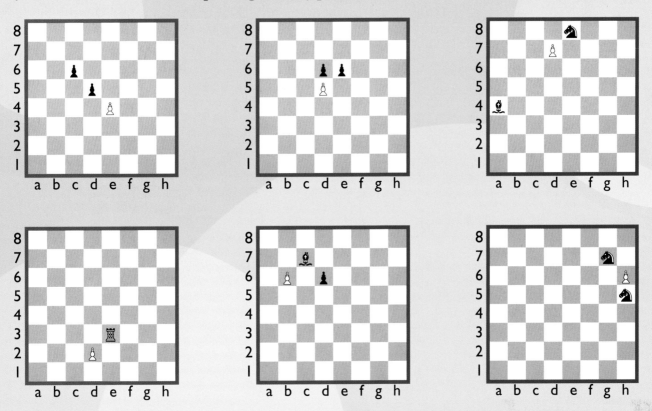

24. "Army of One" Capture all the black pieces with the white pawn, taking one piece each move. (Only the white pawn can move, the black pieces are "frozen.")

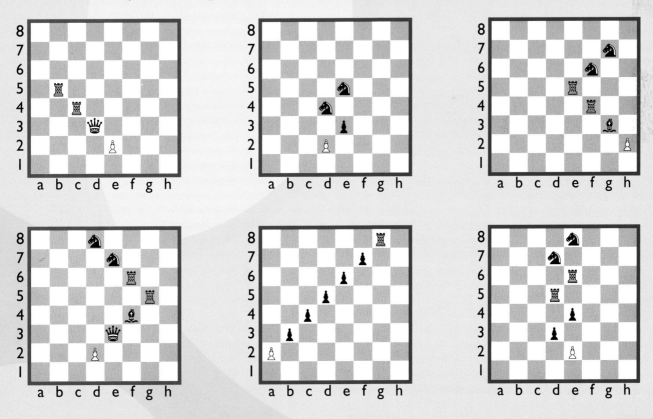

25. "Amazing Maze" Get the white piece to the square marked with a red flag without landing on the mines.

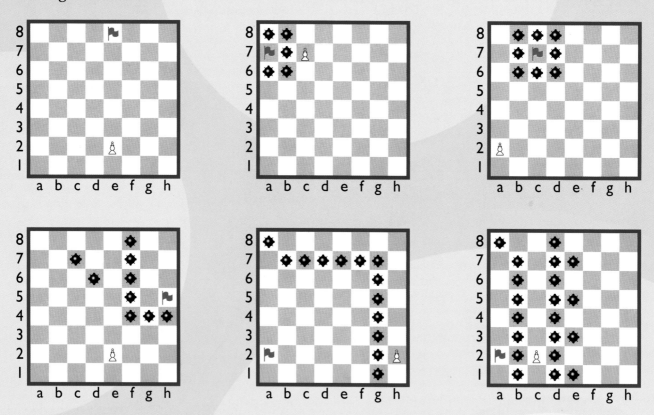

26. "Attack the Enemy" Attack the black piece with the white one.

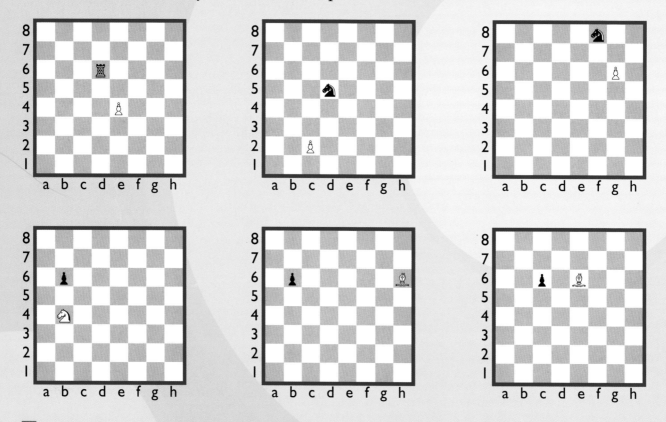

27. "Double Attack" Attack two black pieces with the white one.

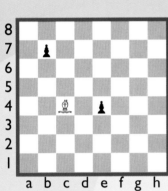

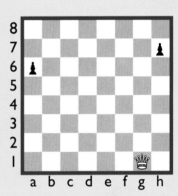

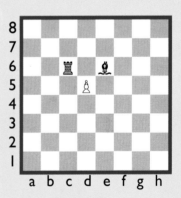

28. Capture a black piece that is not protected.

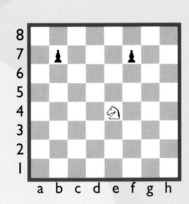
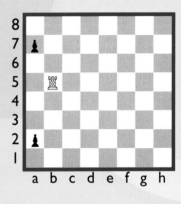

29. "Defense" What move should White make to avoid losing any of his pieces?

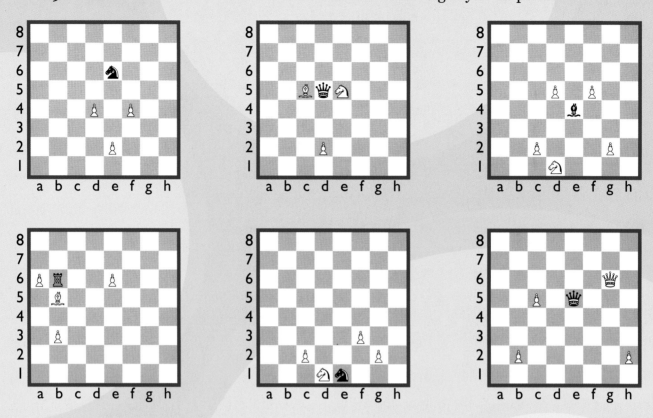

30. "Win a Piece" After which move can White capture a piece next?

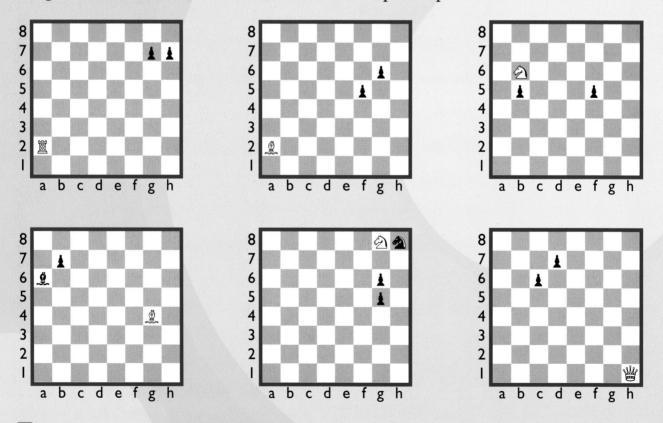

31. "Outsmart the Guards" With the white piece, sneak up to the square marked with a red flag without being attacked by the black pieces.

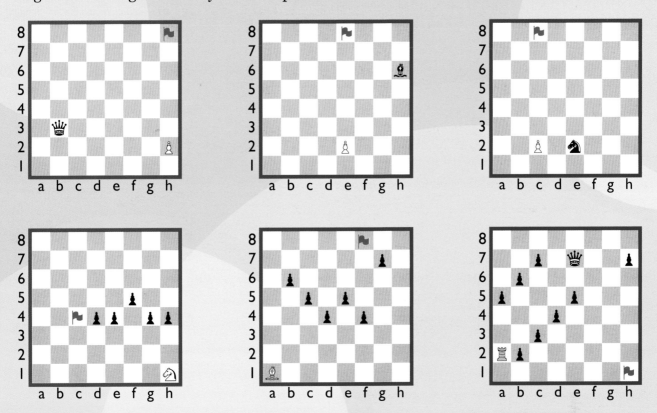

32. "Tied up in Knots" Figure out how the white piece can defeat the black piece by forcing it to be under attack. (White and Black take turns moving.)

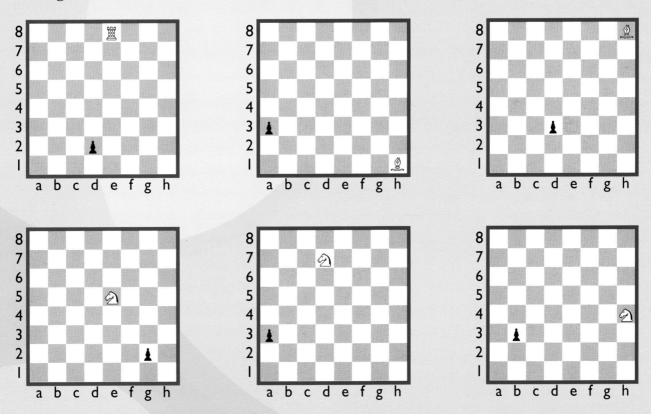

33. Can a single pawn on these diagrams move?

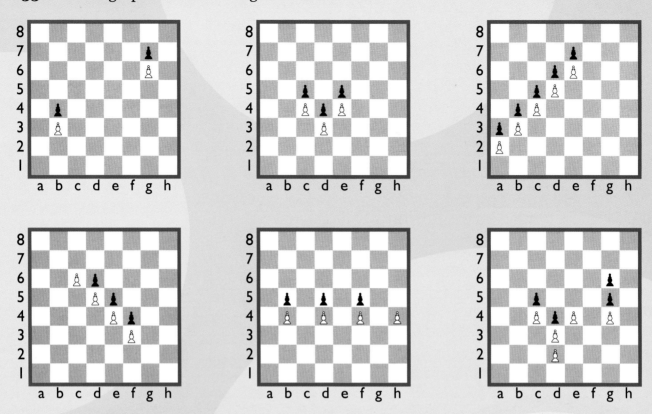

34. "En passant" Move the white pawn two squares ahead. Can the black pawn capture it *en passant*?

Chapter 11

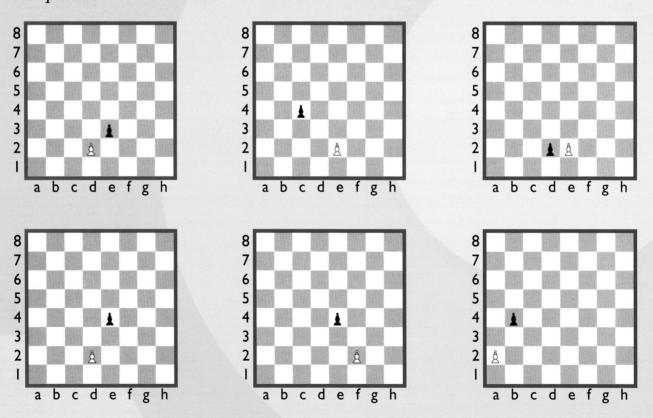

Something was tickling Gary's nose. He woke with a start to find Fred wiggling a blade of grass over his face and grinning.

"Get up, sleepyhead!" Fred urged. "Your friends are waiting for you. It's time to get the notebook!"

"You found it?!" Gary asked.

"Yes, yes, in a way," Fred answered, impatience in his voice. "Now, come on!"

And so the friends headed to the house where Fred told them Zug lived. It was easy to spot, as it looked rather strange on the outside. And also, strangely, they were able to walk right in! Inside the house Gary saw a table with the notebook lying on it. Next to the notebook was a chessboard, the pieces scattered all over. In the corner they saw a bed where Zug lay, snoring loudly.

The kids tried to wake him, but Zug didn't stir.

"I know what to do," Fred said, smiling mischievously. He yanked Zug's pillow out from under his head and dropped it on his face.

Zug woke with a yell, thrashing about but only succeeding in becoming more tangled up in his blankets.

"Help! Who are you? Leave me alone!" Zug babbled as he fought. "Please don't hurt me; I promise never to steal anything again!"

Gary grabbed the notebook and he and his friends left before the mean boy realized who they were.

"I hope Zug learned his lesson," Cassie said, "Maybe now he'll start treating others with respect."

Then they continued on their way. Gary, Cassie, and Riddles went back to continue their lessons, and Fred ran someplace only he knew about.

"Please tell me about the king," Gary asked Riddles as Cassie's trike zoomed toward the Palace.

"The king is the most important piece in chess," Riddles began. "You can play without any other piece, but the king must be on the board all the time."

The group soon arrived at the Palace and walked toward a set of marble stairs.

"Oh, here is the throne room," Cassie said. "His Majesty will tell us more very soon."

The kids climbed up the stairs and entered the throne room. There, sitting on his throne, was a big white King, smiling at Gary and his friends.

"Welcome, welcome!" said the King. "I heard you already know about all the other pieces by now. We kings can go anywhere: ranks, files, or diagonals. But we can only move one square at a time.

"We walk slowly," he added. "Kings shouldn't be rushed."

A little white king got on the board to show Gary all the ways a king can move.

"The king can go to any of the eight squares around him," Gary observed, counting the little king's movements. "But of course, if you are on an edge or a corner, you have fewer choices."

"Very insightful, my most praiseworthy young sir," the King said. "Now, on to capturing. We capture the same way as we move."

A black knight appeared on a square next to the king, and the king captured it.

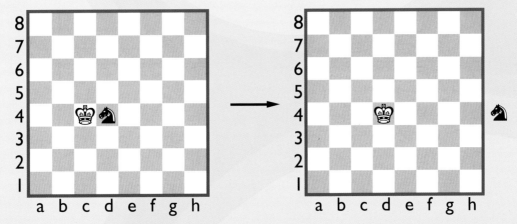

"The king is a very special piece," the big white King continued proudly. "He cannot be captured and taken off the board. You can capture a pawn, a bishop, a knight, a rook, and even the queen, but the king – no. No, no, no."

"Because we are so important, we can only go to squares where we are safe," the King continued. "The king cannot go to a square where he can be captured. Look at the board: in this position I can only go to one square. On the others, I would only face an attack by the black queen."

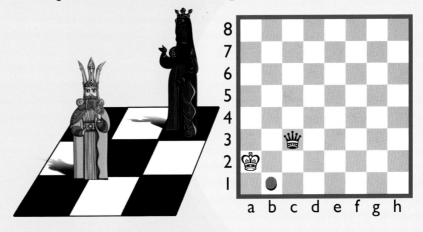

Gary studied the board. The King was correct. There was only one square the little white king could move to that didn't put it in danger.

"Sometimes, and pay attention, because this is tricky, there is a situation in a chess game when the king can jump two squares rather than only one," the big white King continued. "If there are no pieces between the king and his rook on the right, and neither rook nor king has moved yet, the king can move two squares toward the rook and the rook jumps over it. Like this."

And the king pointed at the board.

As Gary watched, the little white king and a little white rook demonstrated the move.

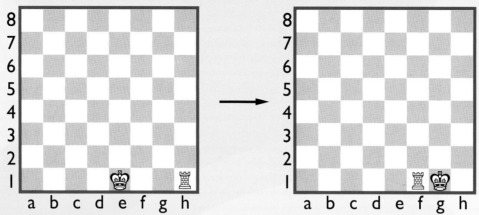

"This is called castling, and it only takes one move for both pieces to get to their new positions," the King explained. "In this example, the king moves to the right, which is called castling short or castling kingside."

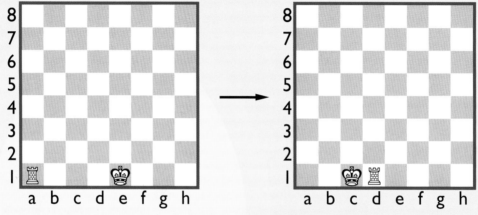

"We can castle to the left side, and that lets the rook jump farther – three squares. That's why it is called castling long or castling queenside."

The King again pointed at the board. "Now the questions: What is the fastest way for a king to move from one corner to the opposite diagonal corner?"

"I know," Gary said happily. "In seven moves, by walking on the long diagonal."

"Correct!" the king said. "Second problem: tell a king how to go around the chessboard and visit all the squares, but only once."

"Easy, the king can move like a rook or a queen," Gary answered.

"Right again. But can you outsmart the guards?"

"I can," Gary said, smiling confidently, as he had solved this problem so many times before.

"Try to get the king to the opposite diagonal corner, without once coming under attack by the dark-square bishop or the queen."

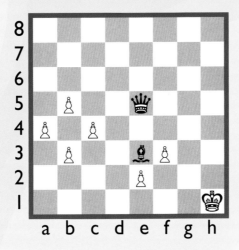

Gary frowned at the board, studying it hard. Was the King trying to trick him?

Solve the Problem of the White King

He studied the board even more carefully, remembering all the ways the opposing pieces could move. Finally, he got through.

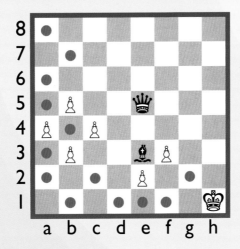

"Very good!" the King said in praise. "You have completed all of your lessons, and passed with flying colors!"

"Will you give me a little king as a present?" asked Gary, and then he blushed, realizing his question was impolite.

"I am already here," squeaked a little white king from Gary's pocket.

PUZZLES FROM THE NOTEBOOK

1. Pick a square, any square! On what squares do the kings move, light or dark?

2. The king is slow, but tell us how he moves: Can a king go from a dark square to a light one? From a light one to a dark one? From a dark one to another dark one?

3. He is the master of all he surveys! How many moves can a king make from a central square? What about a corner square?

4. Despite all the king's horses and all the king's men, is it possible to capture the king in a game?

5. Maybe when nobody's looking, he practices on his trampoline, but can a king jump over other pieces?

6. From White's point of view, which piece is to the left of the white king at the starting position? The right?

7. My kingdom for an answer! How many kings could there be on the board?

8. In the starting position, can either king move?

9. "How do you do?" Can the black king and the white king stand next to each other??

10. "To take or not to take?" Can the white king capture a black piece in these positions?

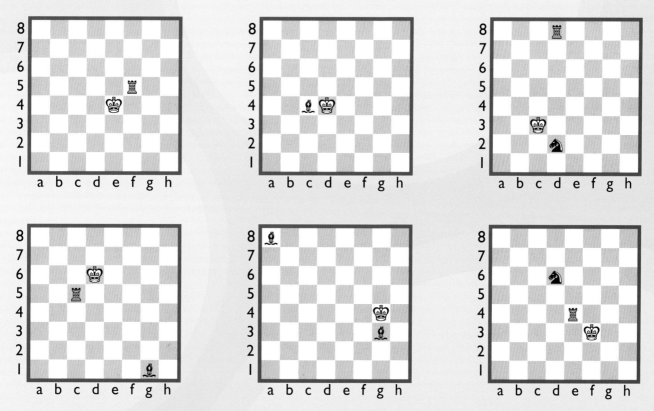

11. "Army of One" Capture all the black pieces with the white king, taking one piece each move. (Only the white king can move, the black pieces are "frozen".)

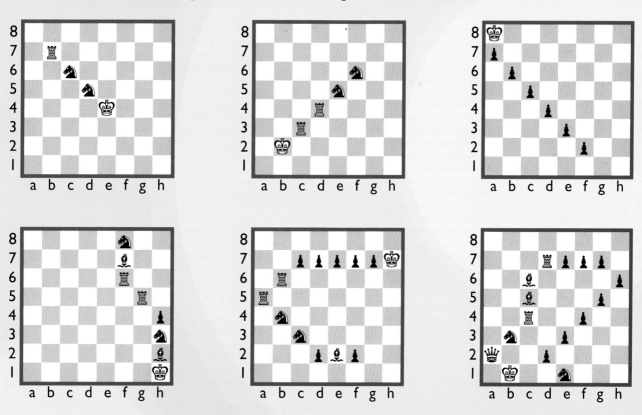

12. "Capture the Flag" What's the shortest path for the white king to capture the flag in these positions?

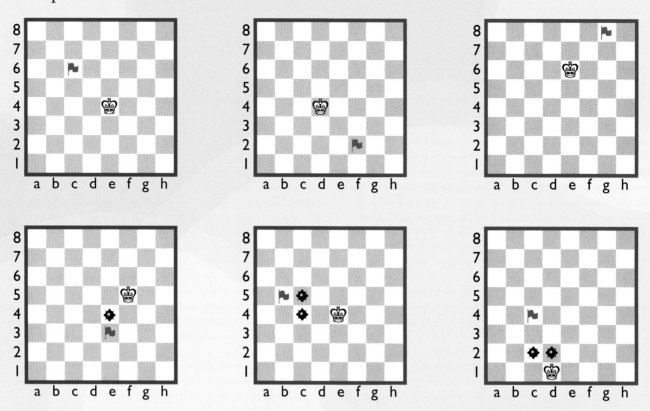

13. "Amazing Maze" Get the king to the square marked with a red flag without landing on the mines.

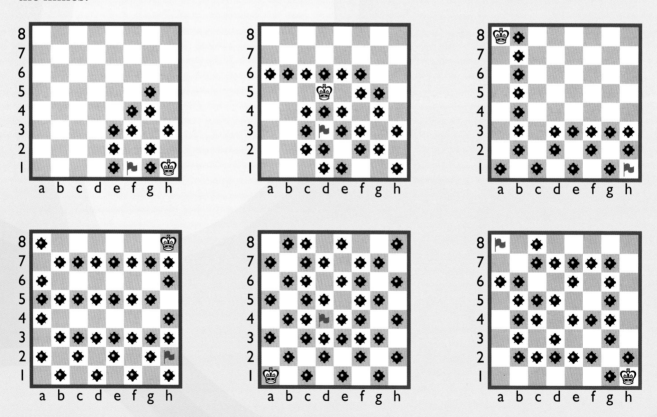

14. "Attack the Enemy" Attack the black piece with the white king.

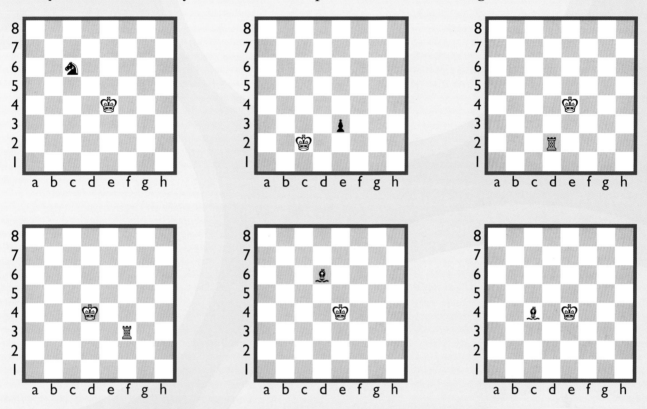

15. "Double Attack" Attack two black pieces with the white king.

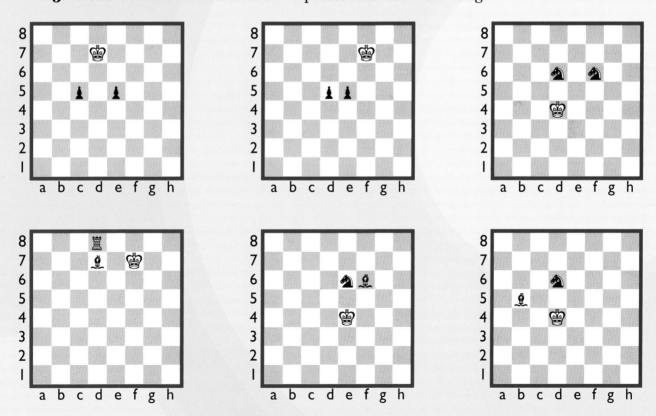

91

16. Capture the only black piece that is not protected.

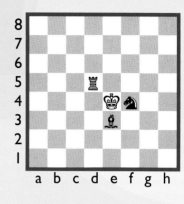

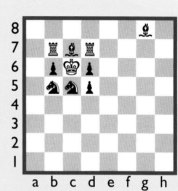

17. "Defense" What move should White make to avoid losing a piece?

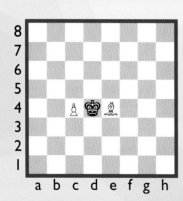

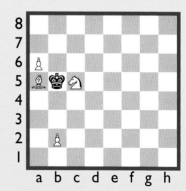

18. "Win a Piece" After which move can White capture a piece next?

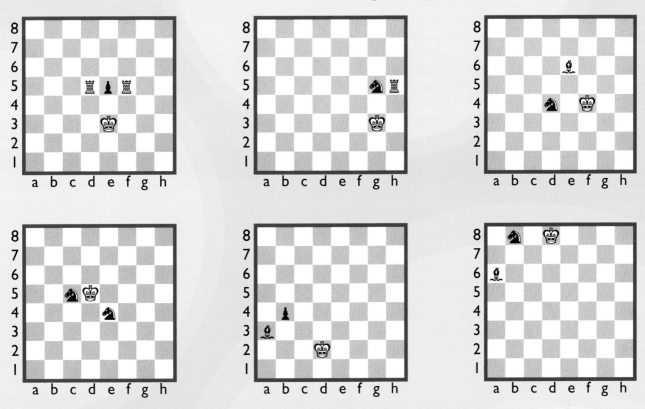

19. "Outsmart the Guards" With the white king, sneak up on the square marked with a red flag without being attacked by the black pieces.

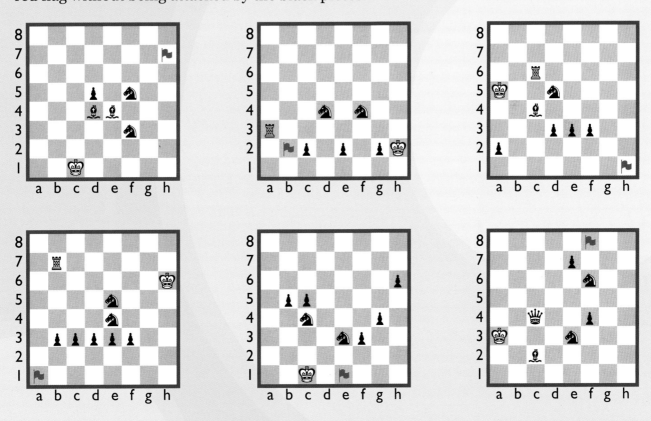

20. "Stealth Fighter" With the white piece, capture the black pieces without being under their attack ("stay off the radar screen") or stepping on the mines.

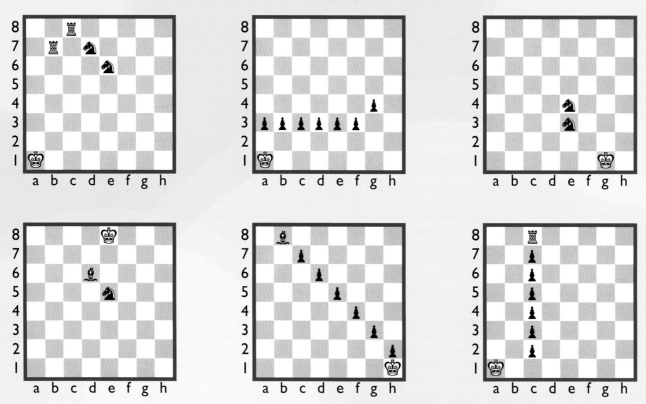

21. "Get to the base" How can White reach the marked square in two moves? (White and Black take turns moving; Black is trying to prevent White from reaching White's goal without putting her own piece under attack.)

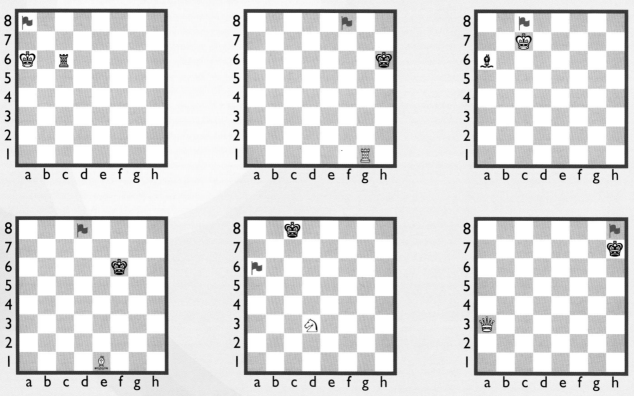

22. "Tied up in Knots" Find how the white king can defeat the black piece by forcing it to be under attack. (White and Black take turns moving)

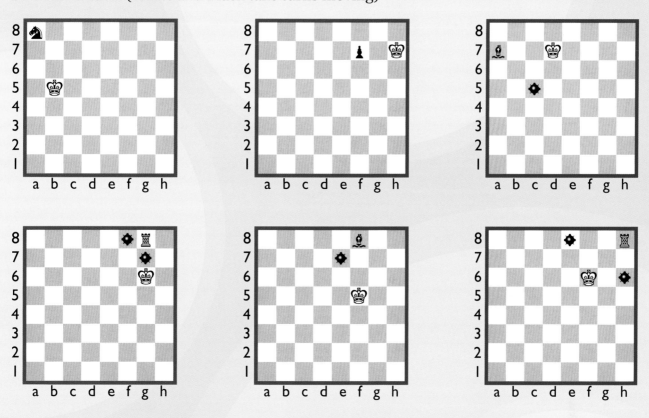

23. Castling – is it possible to castle in these positions?

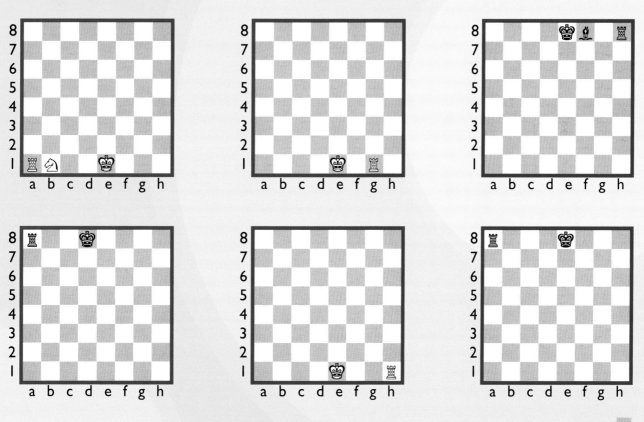

THE FLYING CARPET

Chapter 12

Waving goodbye, the friends left the palace and went to the place where Cassie had parked the tricycle. They were shocked to see the trike gone, with a note left in its place saying, "Hallo frum Zug."

Gary wondered what they were going to do now. Then he heard heavy panting noises, and looked around to see Fred approaching, lugging a huge roll.

"Whew," Fred grunted, dropping the heavy package on the ground. "Just came back from seeing my good old friend, the Black King. He sent you a present, said you might need it soon."

Before they could even thank him, Fred was off again.

"Gotta run, there are so many people I haven't seen in all these years!" he called over his shoulder as he disappeared.

Gary and Riddles unrolled what turned out to be a large rug. It had a chessboard delicately embroidered in the middle. Next to the board, they found a full set of black chess pieces in a small box.

"It is a nice rug," Riddles said, sounding perplexed. "But what are we supposed to do with it?"

Cassie sneezed. "And it could use a good dusting," she said.

There was only one thing to try – he'd seen it in a movie – and Gary hoped it would work in this magical country.

"Everyone, get on," he told his friends. Then, when everyone was aboard, he commanded the carpet. "Lift up!"

The carpet obediently flew up with the kids holding on to it – some holding on tighter than others.

"Where should we go?" Gary asked his friends.

"I know where," Riddles said with that mysterious smile of his, and he whispered something to the carpet that Gary couldn't hear.

The flying carpet soared higher and higher in the sky, made a circle around Caissia and then went east.

"While we are flying, I will teach you about check," Cassie said.

"But we won't be able to set up any puzzles," Riddles grumbled. "We only have black chess pieces."

"What about us?" said the little white pieces from Gary's pocket, in their thin, squeaky voices. "We knew we would be helpful sometime."

Cassie started the lesson:

"Check is when an enemy piece is getting ready to take your king. Look at the board."

"Here the white queen is declaring check on the black king. The king cannot stay under attack even for one move. There are three ways of defending against check. First, you can try to move one of your pieces so that it blocks the attack on the king. Like this."

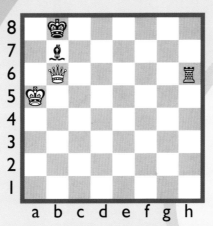

"Second, you can move the king to a safe square. Third, sometimes you can capture the piece that was checking the king."

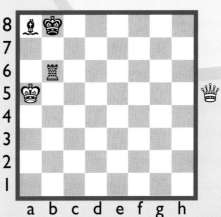

"I would prefer to capture, if I can," Gary said.

"Well, sometimes it is the best way, sometimes it isn't," Cassie said. "You should know how to do all of them. Now, let's practice declaring check on the opponent's king." Cassie set up, in turn, these two positions on the carpet.

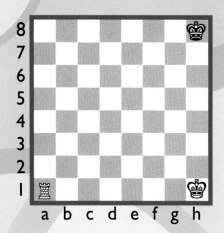

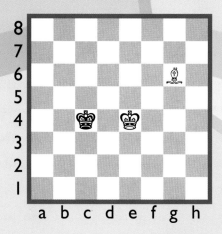

"This is easy," said Gary, having declared check with the rook in the first position, and with the bishop in the second position. Like this:

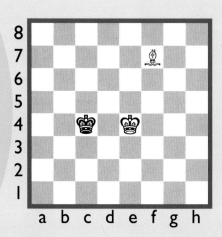

"OK, now find check in these positions," said Riddles. He was always happy to take over the puzzle part of the lesson.

Gary succeeded in both of them. Check! Check!

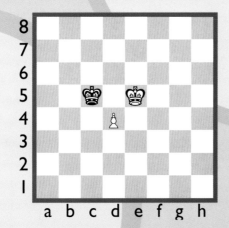 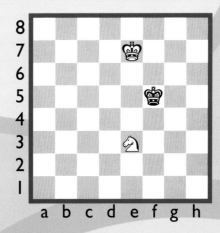

"That was too easy for you," Riddles said, smiling. "Let's find a couple that you really have to think hard to solve."

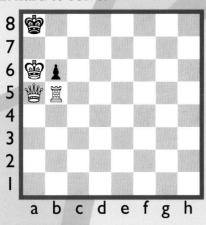 

HELP GARY

Gary struggled with the puzzles for ten minutes before he figured out the answers.

"In the first position, the white king can capture the black pawn and it would be check," he said, studying the board. "In the second, we can move the pawn ahead, clearing the path for the white rook to check the black king."

 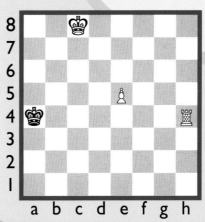

"Correct," Cassie said. "Did you notice that in the first four puzzles, it was the moving piece that declared check?"

Gary nodded, still looking at the board.

"But the last two, it was one piece moving and another piece doing the checking," he said slowly. "The pawn moved, but it was the rook putting the king in check."

"Right!" Riddles said excitedly. "This type of check is called a Discovered Check, and it can be very powerful."

"Can I try a few more?" Gary asked.

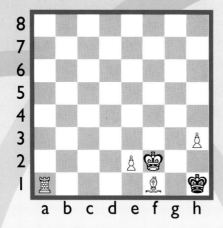 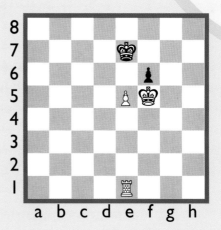

These two were not so hard.

"Amazing. In both positions, two pieces are checking the king at the same time!" Gary said.

 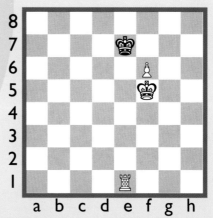

"Right! That's why this type of check is called a double check." Cassie explained. "A double check cannot be blocked by a piece. Also, it can't be stopped by capturing an opponent's piece. The only thing to do here is to escape. Do you think one king can declare check on the other king by moving to the square next to him?"

"I don't think so," Gary said, as he studied the board. "Because you can't move your king into a square attacked by your opponent's pieces. You'd be putting yourself in check also, which is against the rules."

"Wow, you learn so fast!" Riddles said in praise of his friend.

Gary smiled, blushing a bit at the compliment. "Is it always a good idea to check?" he asked.

"No, not always," Riddles said. "But sometimes, checking the king allows you to attack something else, and your opponent can't defend against it because he must protect the king first. Here are some examples."

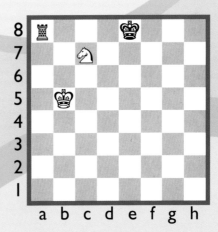

"In the first position," continued Riddles, "the white rook just declared check on the black king. Wherever the king goes, the rook will capture the black queen on the next move."

"That's a big gain!" Gary observed.

"Yes, it certainly is," Riddles agreed. "In the second position, the white knight is attacking both the king and the rook of his opponent. This kind of attack is called a fork. After the black king moves, the knight will grab the rook in the corner."

"Why doesn't the player just castle?" Gary suggested. "That way he could move both the king and rook at once."

"Ah, the King forgot to tell you! You can't castle out of, nor into, check," Riddles explained. "But I like the way you think!"

Gary studied the board some more.

"If castling would put the king in check, this move is not allowed," Riddles continued. "In the next example, if White castles, his king would be under attack by the black pawn. Which means White cannot castle."

"When else can you not castle?" Gary asked.

"If a square over which the king jumps while castling is under attack by the opponent's pieces – that's another time you can't castle," Cassie explained. "Here, if the king were to castle, he would have to go over a square attacked by the light-square bishop. So again, he can't castle!"

"Whew, this is quite a lesson for a carpet ride," Gary said as he scratched the back of his head, his mind spinning with chess moves.

Riddles smiled and said, "Yes, but it's almost over. Here's the last question about castling. Look at the board and tell me this: can White castle in this position?"

"No, he can't," Gary answered. "If White castles, his rook would have to go through a square guarded by the light-square bishop."

"Sorry," Riddles said. "But I understand how you might have missed that.

This is the trickiest rule of castling. Even if the rook goes through a square that would put it in danger, you can still castle. But you can't castle if your king would be moving through check or into check."

The lesson was over, but Gary opened the notebook to make sure he could solve all the puzzles. Can you do them, too?

1. "Castling" Can White castle in these positions?

2. "Check or Not?" Is the black king in check?

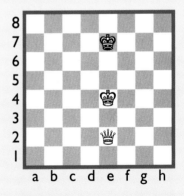

3. Check the black king.

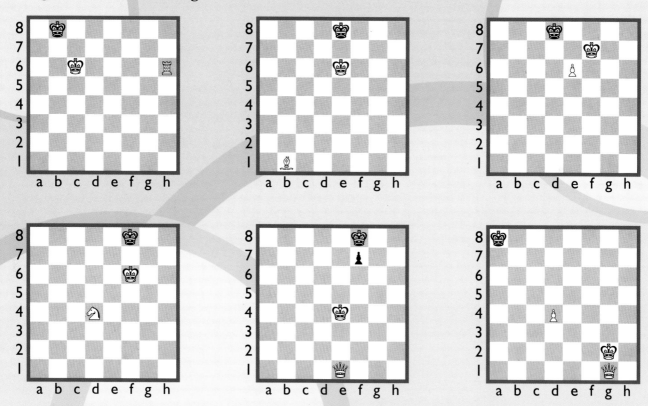

4. "Double Attack" Check the black king and attack the other black piece in the same move. But be careful! Make sure black can't capture your piece!

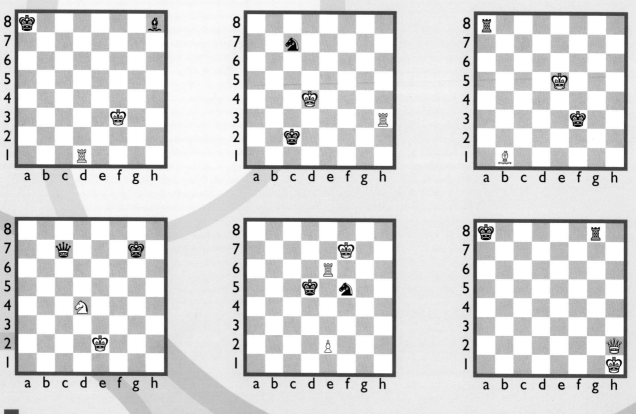

5. "Escaping from Check" The white king is in check. What should you do?

6. "Smart Check" Check the black king, but make sure he doesn't capture your piece.

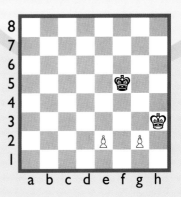

CHECKMATE AND STALEMATE

The group continued on their journey. Gary's head swirled with chess moves as the flying carpet soared over a castle with checkered black and white weathervanes, and landed in the town square of a small village. A big sign on the tallest tower read: Ströbeck.

The town mayor came out to greet the travelers. "Ströbeck welcomes you! Our town is named after a German village, the most famous village in the history of chess. They have been playing chess there for more than a thousand years, after a prince imprisoned in one of the towers taught the villagers how to play."

The mayor shook hands with the travelers, and smiled at Gary as he did so.

"In their honor, we stage an annual celebration of Live Chess," he continued. "On that day, we roll a giant chessboard out onto the main square and our citizens, dressed up in colorful costumes of chess pieces, stage a game. Today, you are in luck! We are having a dress rehearsal for the festival."

He pointed to a group of people struggling to unroll the giant board-rug onto the square.

"I bet you want to know how to end a chess game," he said. "The way to win in chess is to declare a Checkmate or, simply, Mate. When you declare check on your opponent's king, and there is no defense against it, it is called a mate. Checkmate means one king is in check and it has no way (move, take, or block) to escape."

"So whoever checkmates his opponent wins the game?" Gary asked.

"That's right!" the mayor said. "Here are some examples."

He clapped his hands four times, and the people dressed in costumes presented these four positions on the giant board, one after the other.

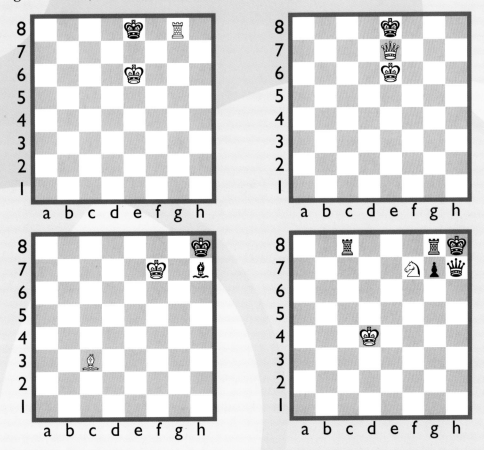

Gary watched the show in amazement. He was especially surprised by the last of the four positions, where the white knight declared the checkmate on the black king.

"How is it possible?" he asked. "Black has so many more pieces, the queen, a rook... and White wins??"

"Ah, but this is an important lesson," the mayor explained. "In chess, like in life, force doesn't always win. It is also about skill. If you check the king and there is no defense against it, you win, no matter how many pieces you have left on the board."

Gary studied the board again as the live chess pieces moved about in various formations. When they came to a stop, Riddles looked at Gary with an expectant look on his face.

"What move comes next, if you are the white army?" he asked his star pupil.

Gary stared hard at the board for several minutes, but couldn't find anywhere to move that wouldn't put his king in check.

Frustrated, he studied the other white pieces. They, too, couldn't move without putting the white king in check!

"You're correct," the mayor said, as if he could read Gary's mind. "It's White's turn, his king is not in check, but White can't move. That is called a stalemate, and the game ends in a draw, which is the chess word for a tie. Nobody wins."

As Gary watched, puzzling through the idea that a game could end with no winner, the live chess pieces moved about in various positions to demonstrate stalemates.

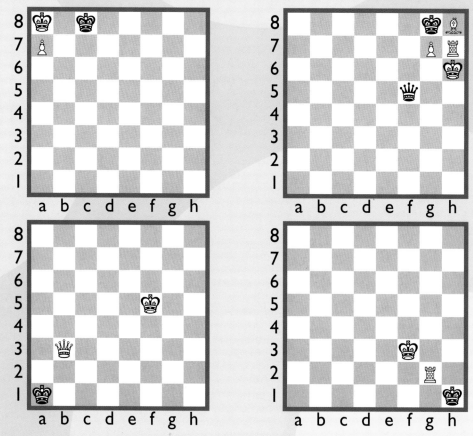

"And if you don't have enough strength to checkmate the king, it is also a draw," the mayor continued.

"*I* have enough strength!" Gary assured him with confidence.

The mayor smiled at Gary. "Let's just see about that," he said, and with a wave of his hands a new position arose on the board. "Find a mate by White in one move here."

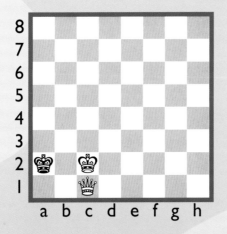 

HELP GARY SOLVE THESE PROBLEMS

"To declare checkmate, you need to attack the king in a way he can't defend," Riddles reminded Gary.

"Yes, I remember," Gary answered. "I must put the king in check and make sure he can't escape, capture the checking piece, or block it."

And Gary happily solved the problems.

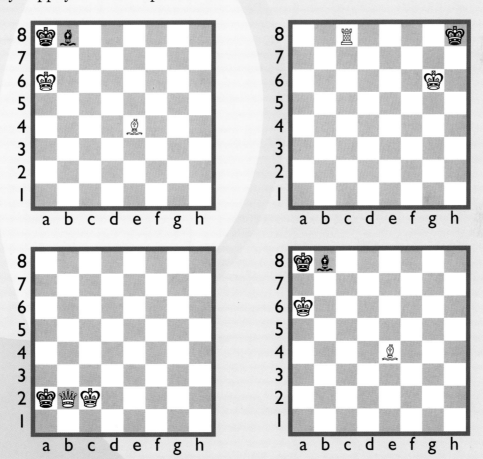

"Very well!" the mayor said. "Now find checkmate in these positions; they are a bit harder."

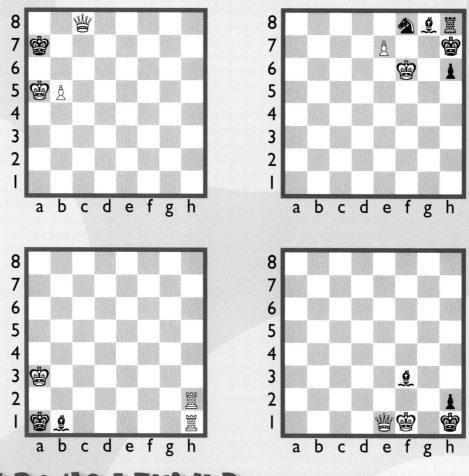

WHAT DO YOU THINK?

This was, indeed, a little harder. In the first position, though, Gary easily found the solution: just move the white pawn and the game is over. He kept looking at the second position, but nothing seemed to work.

He even promoted his pawn to a queen, but it wasn't checkmate; it wasn't even check!

Riddles, seeing the confusion on his friend's face, said to Gary, "I'll give you a clue: remember that the pawn doesn't have to turn into a queen!"

"Aha!" Gary exclaimed, as he found the solution. He used his pawn to capture the black knight, and then advanced the pawn to the eighth rank, where he promoted it to a knight.

"Checkmate!" he declared triumphantly.

In the third puzzle, Gary attacked the king with one of his rooks right away. Except, he thought to himself, was it checkmate?

"Can Black's bishop capture my attacking rook?" he wondered. "No, it can't, because that would put the king in check by the other rook, and you can't do that."

He smiled when he realized that he'd succeeded.

"Checkmate again!" he said.

In the last position, Gary tried to move the queen into all the possible squares; nothing worked.

Then he said out loud to himself: "Maybe I should try using my king?" He moved his king over a square to create a discovered check. And...checkmate!

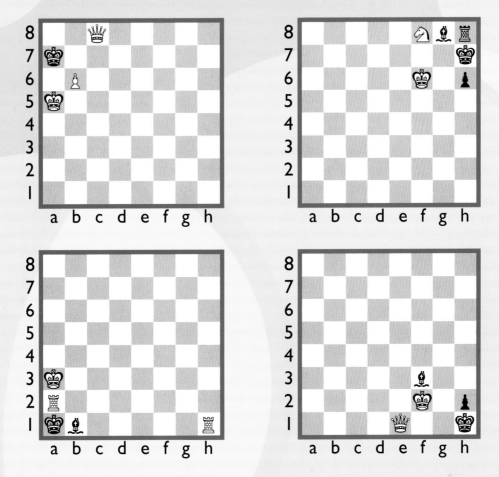

"Great job, my lad," the mayor said in praise. "Here is the last problem: can White declare checkmate in one move?"

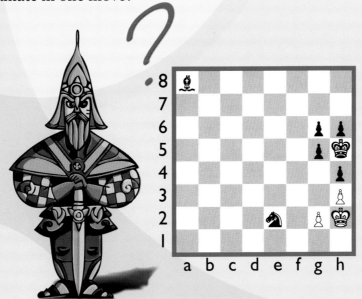

"Sure," Gary said quickly. "Just move the white pawn two squares ahead and it's check. The king can't go anywhere."

Then he realized why it was such a tricky question: "No, wait! White can't do that. If White makes this move with the pawn, Black can take the white pawn *en passant* and it's checkmate for White!"

"Correct," confirmed the mayor. "Now you can checkmate."

"Did you know that the word checkmate comes from the Persian *shah mat*, which means 'the king is defeated'?" Riddles asked Gary.

"Only Riddles could expect other people to know things like that," Gary thought to himself, but he only said, "I know this now. Can we do more checkmate problems from your notebook?"

PUZZLES FROM THE NOTEBOOK

1. Check this one out: what's better, to give check or checkmate to your opponent's king? Is it better to give checkmate or capture the queen?

2. Okay, mate, you ought to know this: Is it possible for White to give a checkmate by moving his queen? His rook? Pawn? King?

3. This puzzle is tough, but you can do it. Set up a position that checkmates Black using only the white king, a white rook, and the black king.

4. "Checkmate or not?" In the positions shown on the board, is it checkmate for the black king?

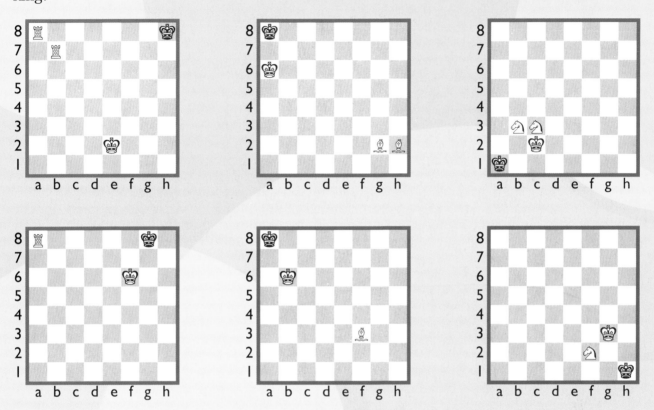

5. "Stalemate or Not?" In the positions on the board, is it stalemate for the white king?

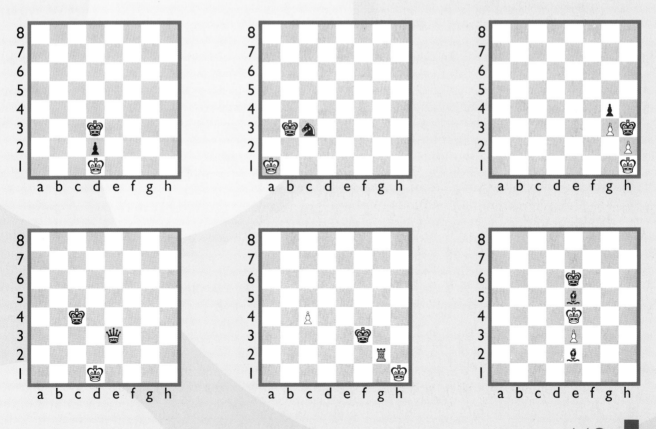

113

6. "Checkmate or Stalemate?" Which one is it?

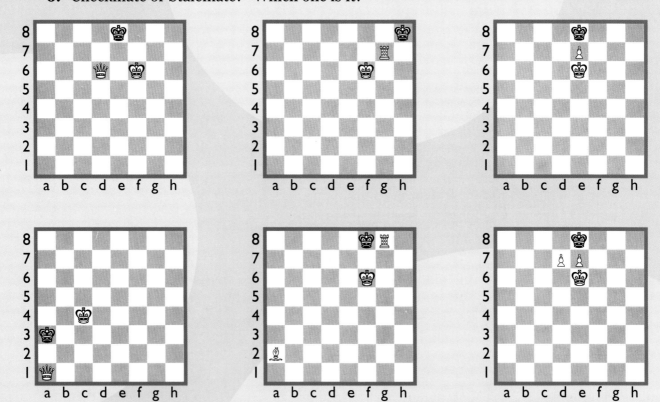

7. "Rook Reaches for Checkmate" White to checkmate Black in one move with the rook.

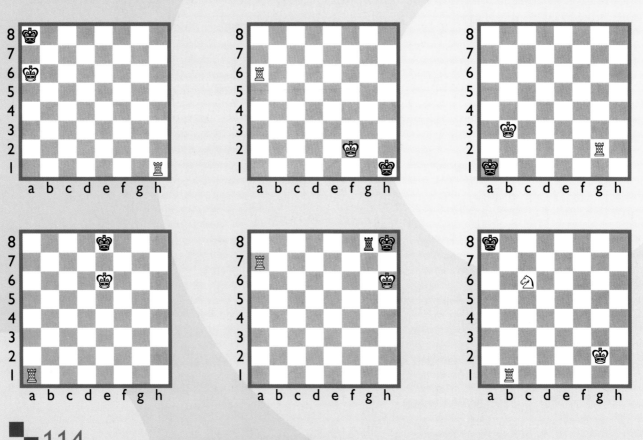

8. "Bishop Bounces Black in Checkmate" White to checkmate Black in one move with the bishop.

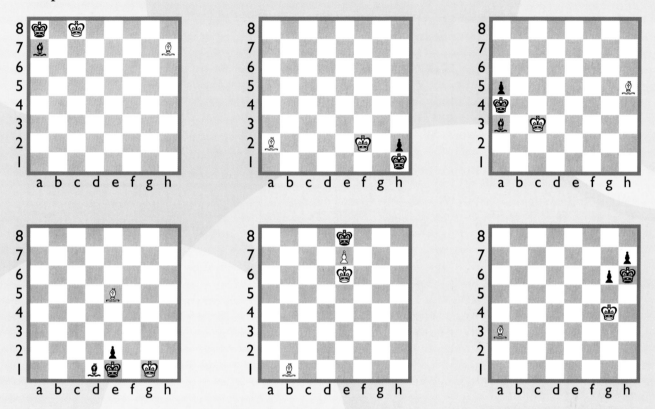

9. "Queen Quietly Checkmates" White to checkmate Black in one move with the queen.

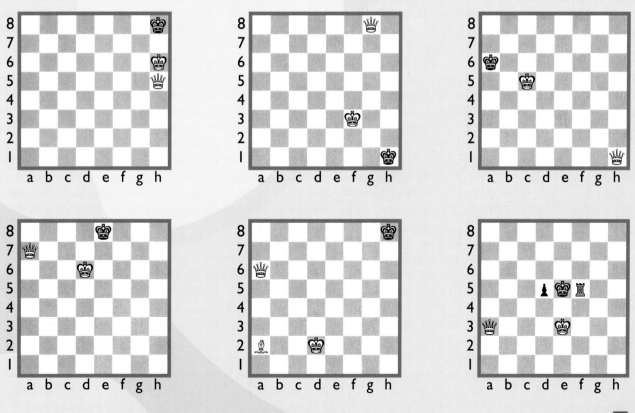

10. "Knight Knocks off a Checkmate" White to checkmate Black in one move with the knight.

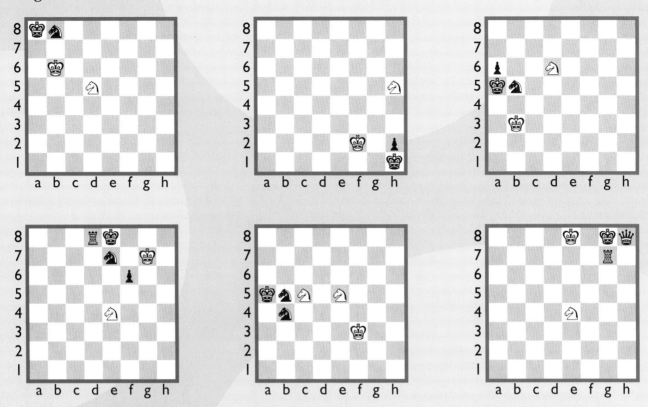

11. "Pawn Punches Its Way to Checkmate" White to checkmate Black in one move with the pawn.

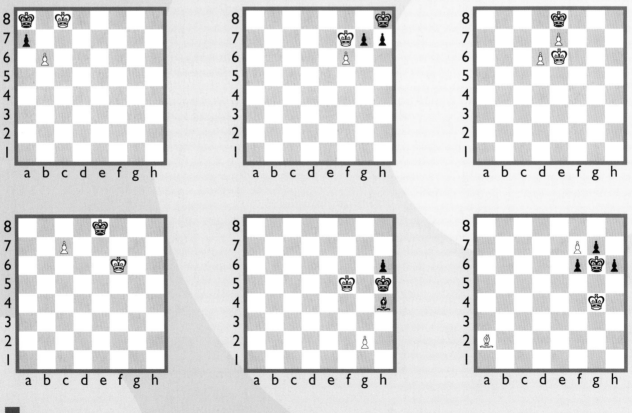

12. " Cool, Clever Checkmate" White to checkmate Black in one move.

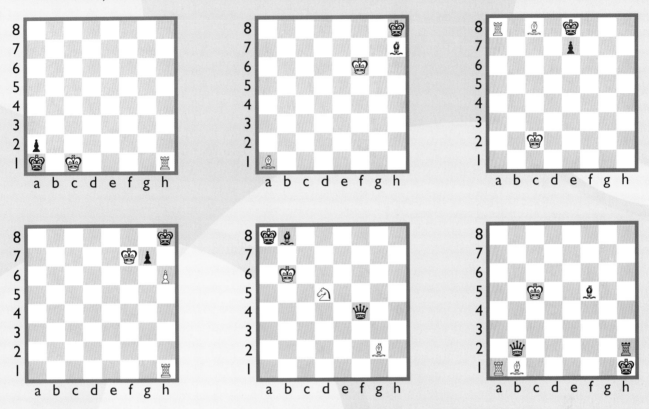

13. "Checkmate Right from the Start" Figure out which side can checkmate in one move and how.

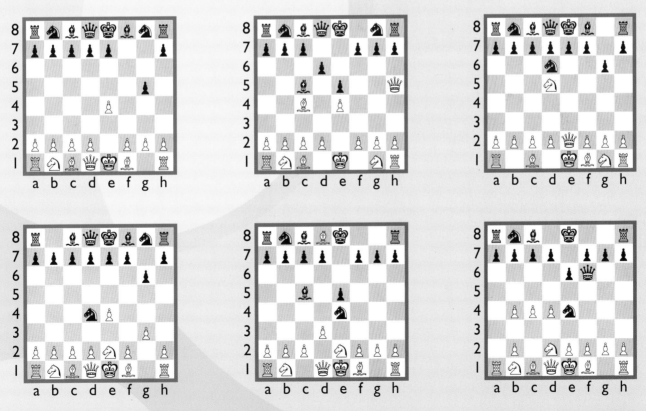

GARY IS SOLVING DIFFICULT PROBLEMS

The friends jumped aboard the flying carpet and headed back to Caissia. Gary was still thinking about the last puzzle. "It's easy to checkmate in one move, but how can I get into a position where I can do it?" he asked.

"That is the really hard part of chess," Cassie said with a laugh. "You can learn, but it will take time and a lot of practice. Look at this position, for example."

"It's White's turn to move. He can't checkmate the black king in one move, that's easy to see. What do you think White should do to win quickly?"

"Simple," Gary said, feeling proud of himself. "Just push the pawn up the file and promote it into a queen. Then, with the queen, you will checkmate."

"No way!" Riddles called out. "If the pawn becomes a queen, it's stalemate!"

"Well, then into a knight or a bishop, or something," Gary mumbled, unhappy that he missed the stalemate.

"A king with a bishop or a king with a knight cannot checkmate the opponent's king without help from other pieces," Cassie said. "Don't try to guess; look at the board and think."

The powerful queen seemed like such an obvious choice when promoting a pawn, Gary thought with frustration. But it wasn't always the smartest move, he realized, looking at the board.

"When you promote a pawn, you need to make sure it's not going to be captured on the next move, and whether or not there is a stalemate," he said slowly, looking at Riddles for confirmation.

Riddles nodded with encouragement. "I'm pleased that you're beginning to think strategically, my friend."

"If you could get captured or be stuck in a stalemate right away, you should think about promoting the pawn into the second strongest piece. That would be the rook," Gary continued.

"Try it and see what happens," Riddles said with his mysterious smile.

Gary studied the board again, between suspicious glances at Riddles. Was this another trick?

He moved the white pawn onto the last rank and turned it into a rook. The black king had only one place to go, and after the move, Gary used his new rook to declare checkmate.

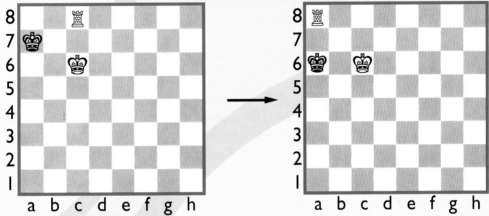

"You know what just happened?" Riddles asked excitedly. "You found a checkmate in two moves!"

Gary was very excited. "I want more puzzles!"

Cassie set up another position on the carpet:

"That's easy," Gary declared. "I'll just check the black king until he has nowhere to go."

"It won't work," Cassie said. "When you are trying to checkmate the opponent's king, it is often useful to limit where he can go, to cut off as many ways to escape as possible. Just make sure there is no stalemate!"

"Yes, I will push him to the edge," Gary announced as he moved the white king diagonally towards the black king. The black king had only one square to retreat to. This is where Gary declared a checkmate. Like this:

Gary sounded surprised. "Now I know you're pulling my leg! You said that a king with a knight can't checkmate. And here Black has a lot of pieces to defend himself!"

"Black's pieces would only get in the way, if you knew how to trick them," Riddles insisted.

No matter how long Gary looked at the puzzle, he couldn't see a solution.

Riddles had to explain: "Black does have a lot of pieces, but they are all stuck and can't move. The move Black can make is with the knight pawn. Here is how you can take advantage of it." And Riddles moved the white king one square lower.

Gary remained unconvinced. With a snicker, he moved the black pawn forward. Now what?

The white knight sprinted and attacked the black king. Checkmate!

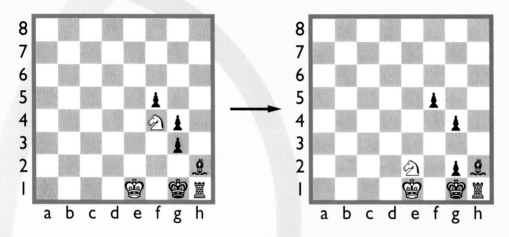

"What a powerful knight!" Gary could barely believe it. "Didn't you teach me that the queen is the strongest piece, then the rook, and the knight and the bishop are at the end?"

"Most of the time, that is true," Riddles agreed. "If you count the strength of a pawn as 1, then the bishop and the knight are worth about 3 pawns, the rook, 5, and the queen, 9."

"Now I see why it's always a good idea to trade any piece for your opponent's queen," Gary said as his mind calculated the numbers. "Or, if you can get your opponent's rook and only give a knight or a bishop, you come out ahead."

"Not always," Cassie replied. "That's the beauty of chess. Sometimes you trade pieces of equal value. But sometimes you give up a stronger piece for a weaker one. Or even for nothing. This kind of sacrifice is called a chess combination. Sometimes you give up a piece to make it easier for you to checkmate your opponent. There are lots of other times when you might sacrifice, but let's work on this one for now."

"You will see some examples as you try to do these exercises. The goal is to mate the opponent in two moves by using a clever combination."

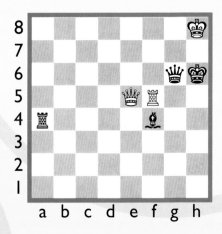

"You need to take the dark-square bishop with the rook on the first move," Cassie instructed. "It wins a whole bishop. And then if Black takes your rook, you can fight back with the queen."

"It is a bad move," Riddles said unceremoniously, and shook his head. "If you try that, YOU will get checkmated right away. Black can just move the queen diagonally to the right and it's checkmate!"

"I can't really come up with anything else." Gary said, his frustration plainly showing on his face.

"Don't despair, it is very hard," Riddles said. "Look, watch this. The white rook declares check on the black king."

"This is silly. Black can just take the rook with his queen" Gary said dismissively.

"True, but after that the white queen can checkmate. See?"

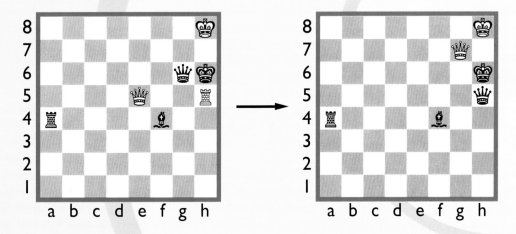

"I see, I see!" Gary said. "You need to give up a piece, and when your opponent takes it, you sneak up on him and checkmate. Right?"

Both Cassie and Riddles smiled at their friend in agreement.

"Please, give me another puzzle? Just one that's a little easier this time," Gary pleaded.

Cassie set up another position on the carpet's board.

DO YOU SEE A CHECKMATE IN TWO MOVES?

"This is a checkmate in one move!" shouted Gary as he moved his queen all the way down to the end of the file. "Checkmate!"

Suddenly he felt butterflies in his stomach and wished he had not been so hasty. "Oh, no, the black rook can capture my queen!"

Riddles and Cassie said nothing to help him. Then Gary brightened. "But then I can take the black rook with mine. Ha! Now it's checkmate."

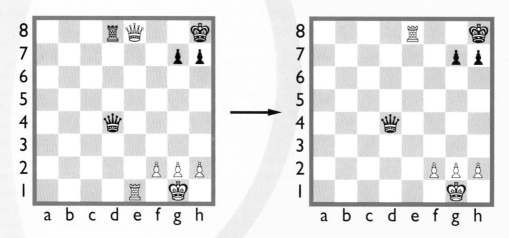

"That's right!" Cassie said. "How about this one? Can you solve it?"

HELP GARY CHECKMATE THE BLACK KING IN TWO MOVES

"Yes, you just have to sacrifice something," Gary said, capturing the black rook with his queen.

"Why would you do this?" Riddles objected. "The black king can take your queen and there is no checkmate in sight."

Gary put the pieces back where they were and tried a different approach: he moved the queen two squares down the file and announced: "Check!"

But Black simply blocked the check by moving his rook between the white queen and his king. Still no checkmate on the next move.

Finally, Gary came up with a different idea – a knight sacrifice. The knight moved to declare check on the black king, and once the pawn captured it, Gary saw the checkmate. Like this:

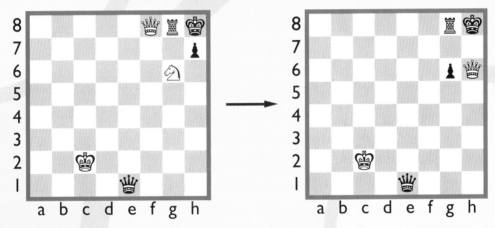

Everybody cheered Gary's success and Cassie came up with another puzzle.

White to Move and Checkmate the Opponent in Two Moves

Check! The white rook rushed to the left. Black had no choice but to capture the rook with the bishop and then White declared checkmate with his only pawn:

125

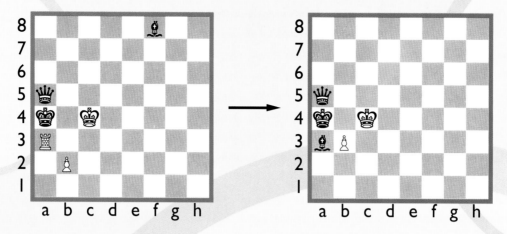

Everybody was happy that Gary solved such a tough puzzle.

Riddles said: "We are approaching Caissia. Do we have enough time for you to solve another puzzle? In this one, Black should checkmate White in two moves."

"Of course we do." Gary overflowed with confidence. He tried to solve the puzzle too quickly by checking the white king with his knight. But the white rook took the knight, and checkmate wasn't even close.

"Don't feel bad, Gary, this one's really hard," Cassie said encouragingly. "This trick is called Smothered Mate. First, the queen declares check and sacrifices itself."

The white rook had to take the queen and then the knight delivered the checkmate.

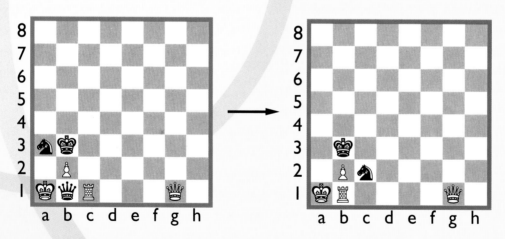

Gary was amazed. "Sweet! Can we do another one?"

"We are about to land, so it's time to pack. I have a lot of puzzles in the notebook that you can solve later," Riddles replied.

Help Gary solve the Puzzles.

126

PUZZLES FROM THE NOTEBOOK

1. Check it out: work out a way that White can checkmate Black in two moves.

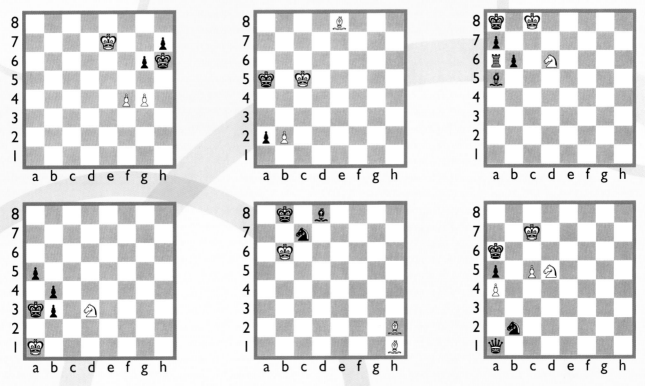

2. Oh, yeah? Black can do that too. Figure out how Black can checkmate White in two moves.

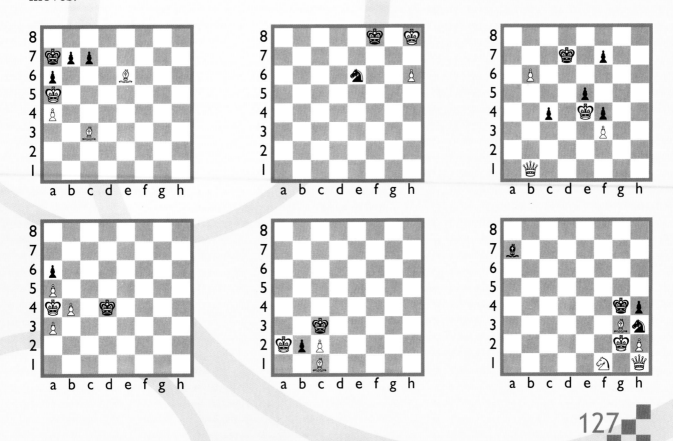

127

3. "'Give Your Rook A Rest' Sacrifice" White gives up a rook and checkmates Black in two moves.

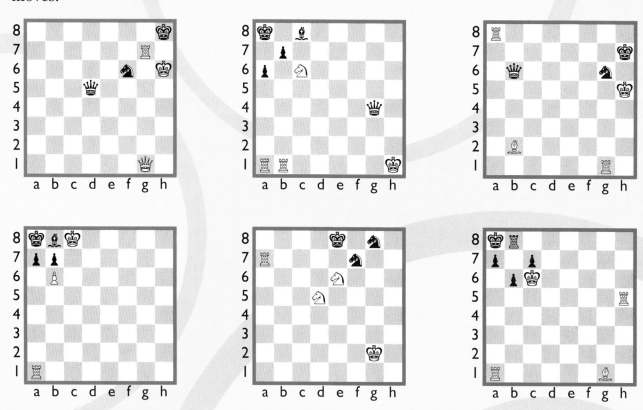

4. "'Trade in Your Bishop' Sacrifice" Black gives up a bishop and checkmates White in two moves.

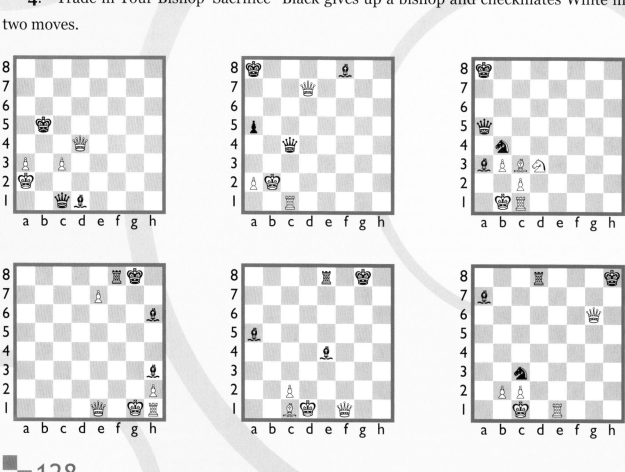

 128

5. "'Pass Up Your Pawn' Sacrifice" White gives up a pawn and checkmates Black in two moves.

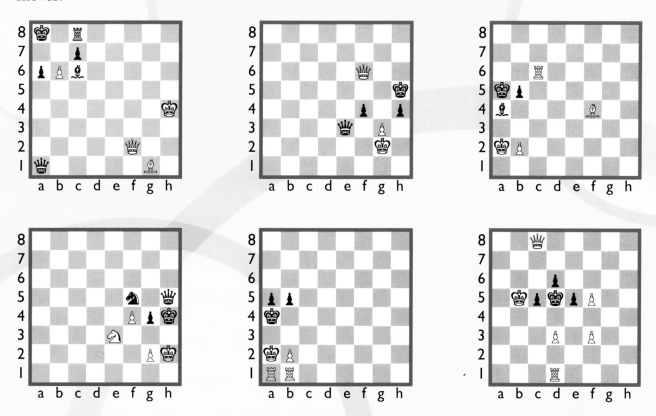

6. "A Noble Knight Sacrifice" Black gives up a knight and checkmates White in two moves.

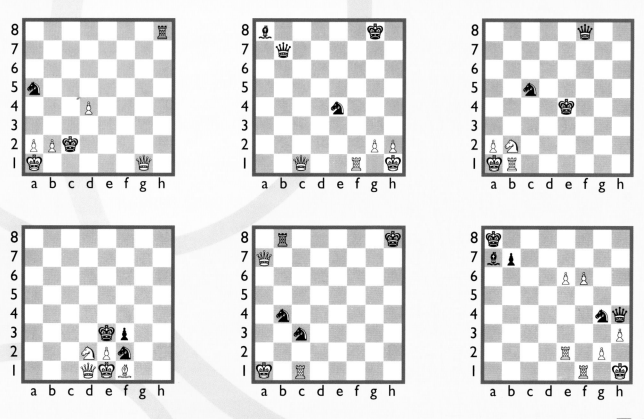

7. "A Quick Queen Sacrifice" White gives up the queen and checkmates Black in two moves

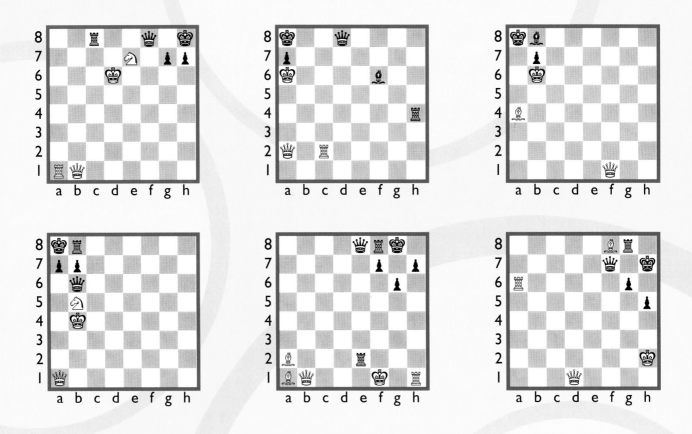

8. "Rook Races to Checkmate" Black to checkmate in two moves using his rook.

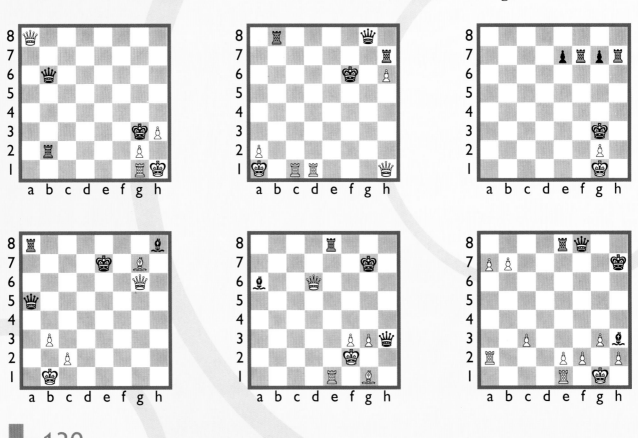

9. "'Wanna Bet That a Bishop Can Checkmate?" White to checkmate in two moves using her bishop.

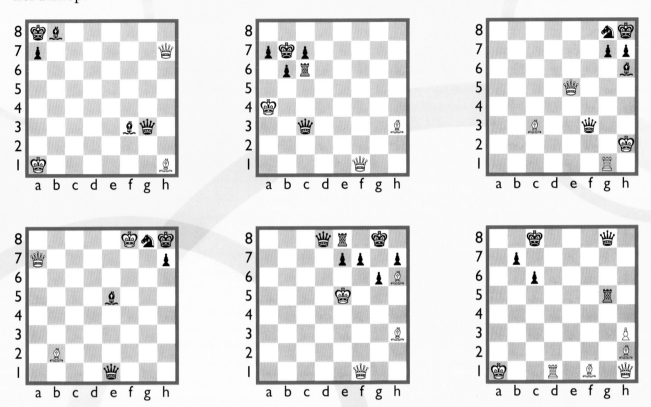

10. "Even a Pawn Can Checkmate" Black to checkmate in two moves using his pawn.

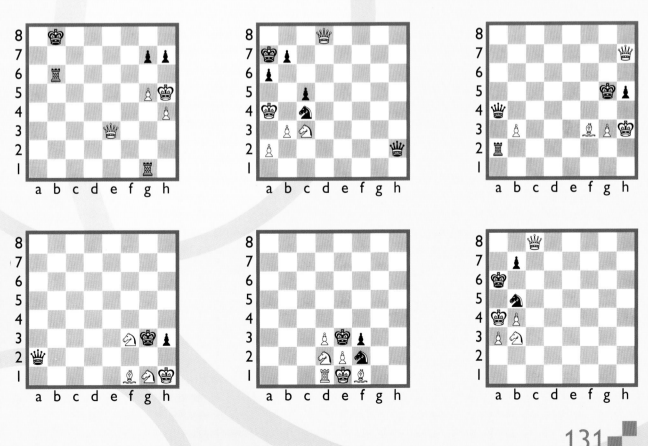

11. "Knight Leaps to Checkmate" White to checkmate in two moves using her knight.

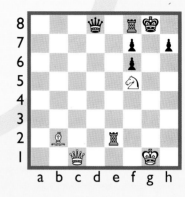

12. "Queen Quietly Checkmates" White to checkmate in two moves using his queen.

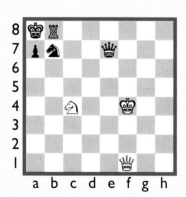

132

13. "Clever Checkmate" Black to checkmate in two moves.

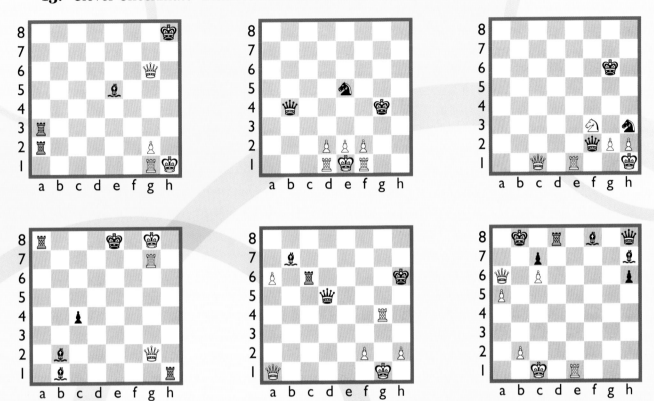

14. "Another Clever Checkmate" White to checkmate in two moves.

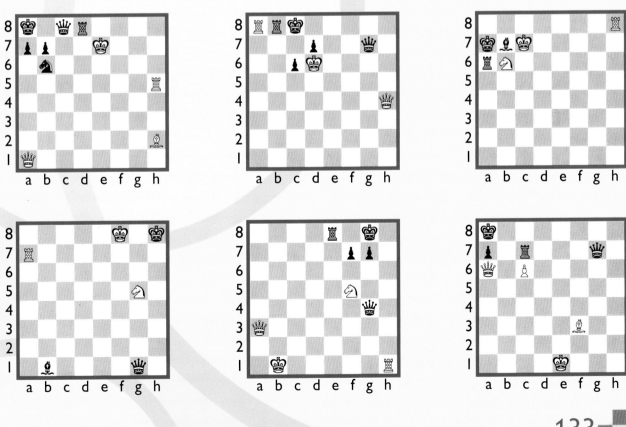

15. "Checkmate Right from the Start" Black checkmates in two moves.

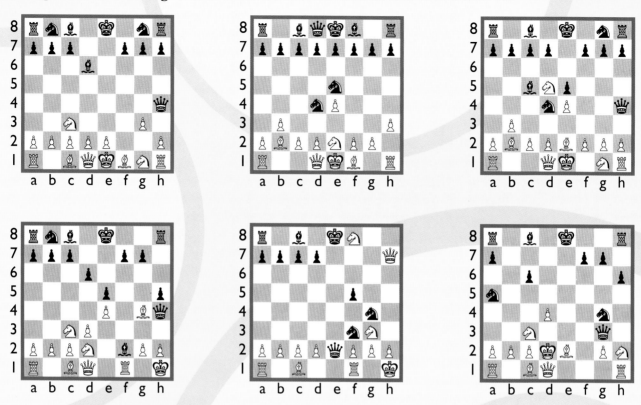

16. "Checkmate Right from the Start, Part Two" White checkmates in two moves.

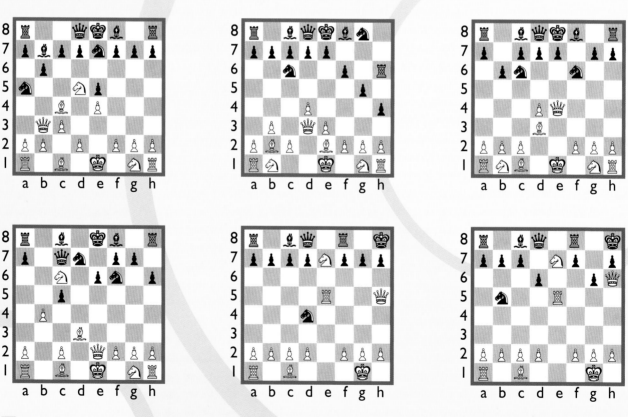

The three friends returned to Caissia and went straight to the palace. The King invited everyone to a feast to celebrate the hard work that Gary had put into learning all the rules of chess. Even Zug came to the party, probably for the free food.

"Congratulations, Gary! We heard that you learned a lot and now know all the moves," the King said, smiling proudly. "My friends here, the Queen, the Rook, the Bishop, the Knight and the Pawn, would each like to ask you a question as the final test."

Zug jumped in. "I also learned a lot! I want to try answering, too."

Cassie and Riddles frowned.

But the king was kind and fair. "You boys can take turns answering questions, if you want," he replied.

The Rook started with the first question: "Over what piece can I jump?"

"That's easy, the king, when you castle," Zug answered quickly.

"That's right. Gary, what piece can never reach the first rank?" the Pawn asked.

"The black!" Zug blurted out of turn. "It is way too far for him."

"A white pawn; they can't go backwards," Gary calmly corrected him.

"Very good!" the Bishop said. "What piece can never land on a black square?"

THINK ABOUT THE ANSWER!

Zug was silent; he didn't seem to know the answer, but probably didn't want to admit it.

Gary decided to help him. "A light-square bishop," he said confidently.

"Right. What piece has an L-shaped move?"

"The knight." This was easy even for Zug.

"What chess piece can move like both the rook and the bishop?"

"The Queen," Gary and Zug answered at the same time.

"Can I jump over a square?" asked the King, winking at the boys.

"When you are really scared?" Zug guessed weakly.

"When you are castling," Gary corrected him again.

Zug narrowed his eyes at Gary. He looked like he was itching for a fight. "I may not know all these silly questions, but I can beat you at chess. Let's play!"

Gary was hesitant. "I can try, but I don't really know how to always win."

To Gary's surprise, the King laughed a great laugh. "And this is great, that you don't know," he said. "Nobody knows. Otherwise, playing wouldn't be fun. And chess should always be fun."

"But I don't want to lose!" Gary said, then pointed to Zug. "Especially not to him."

"If you never lose, what fun is it to win?" the King said. "Now, let me announce the rules. You are going to play three games. Remember, no talking during the game. Carefully think before making each move. If you touch one of your pieces, you have to move with it."

"This rule is called Touch – Move. If you touch your opponent's piece while starting to capture it, you have to take it, even if it means that you are giving up a better piece for it. If you move your piece to a square and let it go, the move is over! No take backs!"

"What if a piece gets knocked over or slides around? How do I fix it?" Gary asked.

"Just say, 'adjust' first, and then move the piece to the center of the square," the King explained.

In the first game, Gary started by moving the knight pawn on the king's side, full speed ahead. Zug responded by pushing his king pawn two squares.

Gary thought for a while and decided to defend his pawn, just in case. For that, he moved the neighboring bishop pawn one square. Like this:

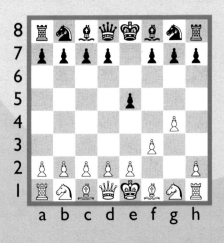

Check! Zug moved his queen and attacked the white king.

"That's checkmate." Gary's face turned red.

"One-zero, Zug leads!" announced the King.

"It was...an accident," Zug admitted shyly, much to Gary's surprise. "I didn't realize it would be checkmate."

For the second game, Zug played with the white pieces. On the third move, he advanced his queen and gave Gary a sly look.

DO YOU SEE WHAT ZUG IS THREATENING ?

"The white queen and the bishop are attacking the same pawn next to my king," Gary thought to himself. "If I ignore the threat, it will be another checkmate."

He moved his knight pawn to put the white queen in danger of being captured.

Zug chuckled and his queen retreated two squares diagonally, still threatening the same pawn as before.

WHAT SHOULD GARY DO?

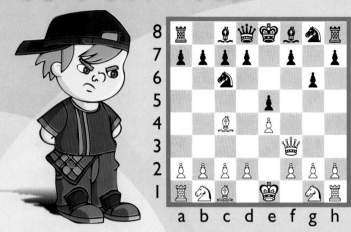

Gary decided to move his other knight and put it between the white queen and the pawn in danger. At least for now, his king was safe.

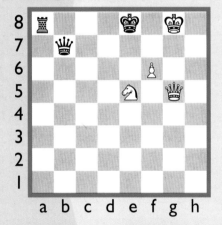

The chess battle between the two boys went on until they reached the following position:

It's Black's turn to move. What would you do?

"Checkmate in one move!" declared Gary.

"No way!" Zug was bug-eyed with surprise. "There is nothing you can do here."

"Oh yes, I can!" said Gary with triumph, and he castled queenside. Checkmate!!

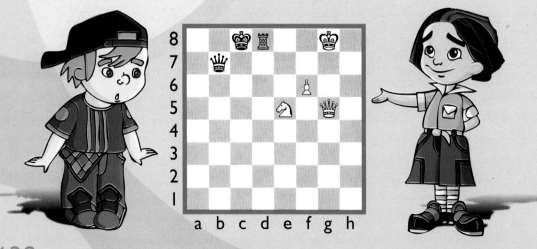

"One-one. Now for the deciding game," the King declared.

"Can I play with white again?" Zug asked.

"All right," Gary agreed.

It was a long, hard battle, and by the time the two boys arrived at the following position, Gary had one extra pawn. Was it enough for a victory? And Zug was attacking his bishop. Gary sank into deep thought for a while.

WHAT DO YOU THINK BLACK SHOULD DO?

Then, to the surprise of everyone watching the game, Gary moved his rook three squares to the left and captured Zug's pawn.

"Now Zug will capture the black rook with his knight," Riddles muttered to Cassie with great disappointment in his voice. "How could Gary miss something so simple?"

This is exactly what happened. Zug quickly snatched up the black rook and gave his opponent a look of supremacy. But with a mysterious smile, Gary moved one of his pawns.

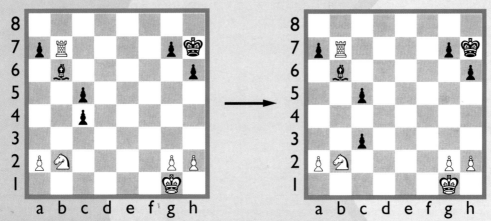

Now Gary's pawn was trying to capture the knight and get close to the first rank, where it could be promoted.

Zug chose the only place for his knight to jump where it could still stop the black pawn.

He moved the knight two squares to the right and one square up.

In response, Gary moved the other pawn on the same file. The pawn threatened the knight, and opened up an attack of the bishop on the white king – a discovered check!

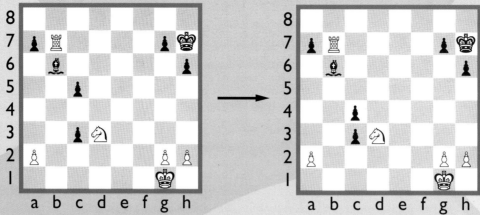

If Zug's king retreated now, Black would take the knight, and surely, one of the pawns could reach the line of promotion! But Zug didn't waste time moving his king. He answered with a clever move that Gary thought he must have prepared in advance.

Zug took the bishop with his rook:

WHAT SHOULD GARY DO?

If Black captures the rook, the white knight could retreat onto the first rank, and Gary's pawns would be blocked forever. "There's a better choice," Gary thought. "I'll take the knight!

Now everyone realized that no matter what Zug did, one of the black pawns could become a queen. And after that, victory would be in sight.

Zug realized it too.

"I wanted to make a different move!" Zug shouted. "Let me try it!"

"It is against the rules to take back moves," the King said sternly. "Please, play on."

Gary again pitied Zug. "What position do you want to go back to?"

"To this one. I shouldn't have moved the knight here. I had a better choice."

And instead of moving his knight, Zug captured the black bishop right away.

"Why did you allow Zug to go back?" Riddles grumbled. "Now he is going to win."

Cassie and the big pieces standing around only shook their heads helplessly.

WHAT SHOULD GARY DO?

It would be a bad move now for Black to take Zug's rook or knight. If Gary took the knight with his pawn, the white rook would capture that pawn and win easily.

If another pawn captured the rook, then the knight would jump, like before, two squares to the right and one up, and block the pawns. Moving the pawn from the third rank to the second wouldn't work either; the knight would only stop it again. And here, without knowing it, Gary made perhaps the most amazing move in the history of chess – he quietly pushed the pawn from the fifth rank to the fourth. Like this:

Everybody was mesmerized. The knight can't take the black pawn because the ther one will advance to the last rank and be promoted to a queen.

If the rook leaves its file, Black can capture the knight and promote the pawn. Now the black pawn closest to the first rank is threatening to march on.

Zug frowned, looking at the board, and came up with a not-so-bad move of his own; he slid his rook two squares down the file. Cassie and Riddles were looking at the board, and from the looks on their faces, they couldn't quite understand who was winning. Gary still couldn't take the knight with his pawn, or the white rook would capture that pawn for an easy win. But Black can't move his pawn forward either, since Zug's rook will take the pawn next to it first, and then all the rest.

Zug proudly addressed the spectators: "I am winning!"

"Not so fast," Gary thought. Then he made another stunning move – he pushed his rook pawn two squares ahead, attacking the white rook.

For several minutes Zug stared at the chessboard with a confused expression.

Riddles leaned toward Cassie and whispered, "Zug has an extra rook and a knight, and Gary has nothing but pawns. Zug probably thinks he's got this in the bag, but he is wrong. If the rook takes the pawn, then Black will capture the knight and promote the pawn on the next move. Zug is out of moves!"

Finally, Zug settled on a move and took a pawn with the knight. In response, Gary pushed his pawn ahead:

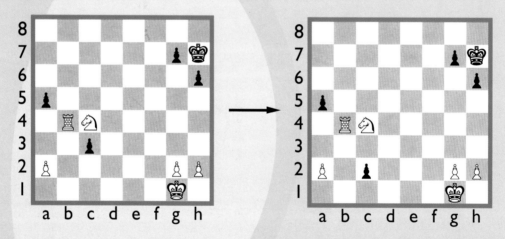

Zug, with desperation in his eyes, captured one more black pawn with his knight. Gary moved his pawn ahead and promoted it into a queen. The new queen was already threatening the white king. Check!

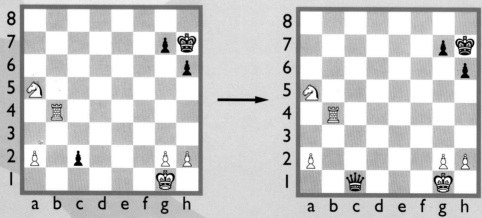

The white king had only one safe square to land on. Once Zug moved it, Gary slid his queen diagonally to the second rank. Check again!

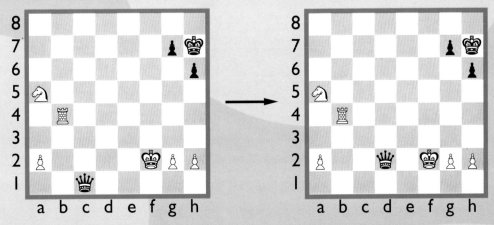

In this position, Gary had forced Zug to ignore his other pieces and move the king. With his next move, Gary captured the white rook.

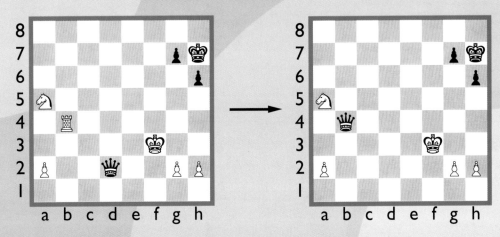

Zug, scanning the board, must have realized that Gary would soon defeat him.

"I give up," he said, on the verge of tears.

"Thank you very much, boys, for a marvelous game of chess," the King said. "We all had a lot of pleasure watching you play."

"To me, it doesn't matter who won," Gary added. "Playing chess with you was a lot of fun, Zug. And a real challenge. I hope we'll get to do it again soon."

Zug eyed him suspiciously, waiting for some kind of insult. But when one didn't come, he appeared to relax a bit, and studied Gary for a moment.

Then Zug smiled as if he'd just made an important decision.

"Thank you," he said. "And I'm sorry for tying you up, and stealing the notebook, so thank you for giving me a second chance. Because you were so cool about it, I'm going to study chess honestly, practice a lot and not cheat anymore. That way, next time you come, I'll beat you fair and square."

"Just you try," Gary said, smiling back at Zug.

Then Gary realized that his friends were looking at him with sadness.

"We enjoyed having you here, my bright young lad," said the King. "But unfortunately, it is time for you to return home."

Zug brought the magic tricycle while everybody said goodbye to Gary.

Riddles, after shaking Gary's hand, gave him a present: his amazing notebook full of puzzles.

"No way," Gary said. "You want me to have this?"

"You've earned it," Riddles said, "because you worked so hard."

Gary thanked him and reluctantly got aboard the tricycle. But Cassie didn't get in.

Gary looked sad. "Aren't you taking me back?" he asked. He'd hoped to spend the trip home talking to her more about chess.

"Not this time. But the tricycle will get you home safely." As she said this, the magic trike started to take off.

"Play lots of chess and have fun!" Cassie said, waving at him. "I am sure we will see you again."

As the tricycle zoomed away, Gary continued to wave as his friends grew smaller and smaller, like little ants, until they disappeared. Then, his mind swirling with everything he had learned in Chess Country, he leaned back to enjoy the ride.

He'd be home soon enough. And maybe if he taught the babysitter how to play chess, then he wouldn't be so bored! But first, he should really do a few more puzzles. Just to make sure he'd remembered all of his lessons.

1. "White Wins a Piece" What move should White make to capture a black piece on the next move?

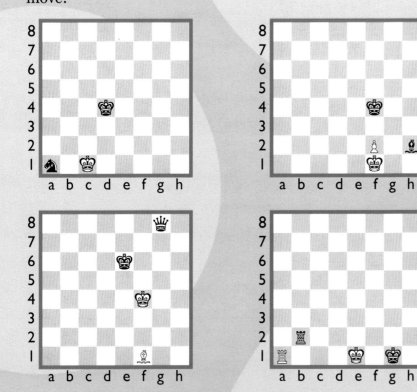

2. "Black Wins a Piece" What move should Black make to capture a white piece on the next move?

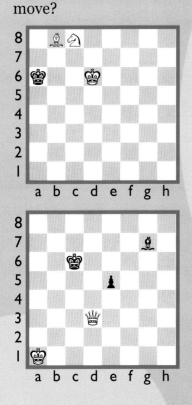

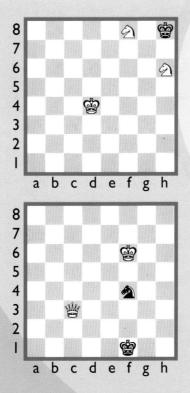

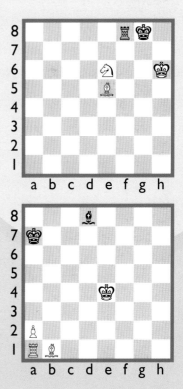

3. "Head-Scratcher" White checkmates in three moves.

CHESS NOTATION

The number of books on chess is greater then the number of books on all other games combined. Yet, chess books would be few and far between if there were not an efficient way to record the moves of games. Chess notation provides for a way to communicate the chess moves. Each square has a name taken from the intersection of the file and rank the square is on.

8	a8	b8	c8	d8	e8	f8	g8	h8
7	a7	b7	c7	d7	e7	f7	g7	h7
6	a6	b6	c6	d6	e6	f6	g6	h6
5	a5	b5	c5	d5	e5	f5	g5	h5
4	a4	b4	c4	d4	e4	f4	g4	h4
3	a3	b3	c3	d3	e3	f3	g3	h3
2	a2	b2	c2	d2	e2	f2	g2	h2
1	a1	b1	c1	d1	e1	f1	g1	h1

a b c d e f g h

The pieces are abbreviated by a capital letter, like this:

R – Rook; B – Bishop; N – Knight; Q – Queen; K – King.

Pawns are not indicated by a letter, but by the absence of such a letter. (In chess books symbols are used instead of letters: Q – ♛, K– ♚, R – ♜, N – ♞, B – ♝.)

Each move of a piece is indicated by the piece's letter, plus the coordinate of the destination square. For example: 1 ♘f3 d5.

When you capture with a piece, put an "x" between the name of the piece and the capture square: 1 ♕xh1.

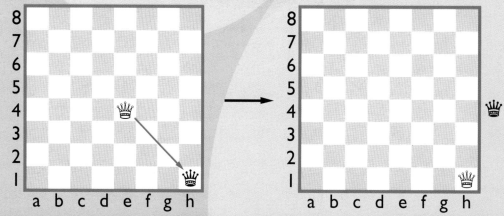

A pawn capture is written as the file the capturing pawn stands on, followed by an x, and the square the capture takes place on – 1...dxe4.

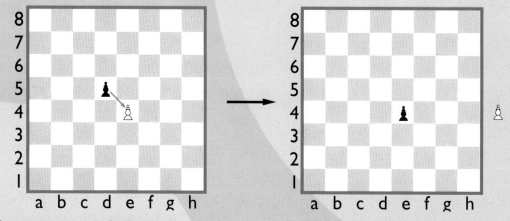

Other Moves and Signs

Castling is denoted differently depending on which side the king has castled to. Castling kingside is represented by 0-0, while queenside castling is notated with 0-0-0.

Pawn promotion is shown by adding ( ) and the abbreviation of the piece the pawn is promoting to: b8(Q)

Check is indicated by + after the move: ♖d4+; double check by ++ after the move: ♗e7++

Mate is shown by the # symbol: ♘d3#.

En passant capture is indicated by e.p. after the move: cxd3 e.p.

In addition to writing the moves themselves, chess players will comment on the strengths and weakness of chess moves with chess move annotation symbols. Here are some common ones:

!! – brilliant move

! – good move

? – bad move

?? – terrible move/blunder

Answer Key

Chapter 1 1. They are equal. **2.** Square. **3.** Chessboard. **4.** Chessboard.

Chapter 2 1. Opponents sit opposite each other. The corner square on the right of each opponent is light. **2.** Eight. **3.** Eight. **4.** Eight. **5.** Eight. **6.** They are the same length. **7.** No. No. **8.** No. No. **9.** Four. Four. **10.** Four. Four. **11.** There are equal numbers of dark and light squares. **12.** No.

Chapter 3 1. Eight. **2.** Eight. **3.** They are the same length. **4.** Two. **5.** Yes. **6.** No. **8.** Square. **9.** Two. Two. **10.** No. **11.** No.

Chapter 4 1. Eight black pawns and eight white pawns. **2.** Two black knight and two white knights. **3.** Two black bishops and two white bishops. **4.** Two black rooks and two white rooks. **5.** One black queen and one white queen. **6.** One black king and one white king.

Chapter 5 1. One. One. Two. Two. Same for Black. **2.** Eight. Eight. **3.** The most common are pawns. Kings and queens are the rarest. **4.** Rooks. **5.** Black. White. White. **6.** First and second. **7.** Eight. Eight. **8.** Eight. Zero. **10.** Eight pieces on first, second, seventh, and eighth ranks. Zero pieces on ranks three through six. **11.** Yes. Four. **12.** There are no such files. **13.** The longest diagonals have the most chess pieces. **14.** No. No. No. **15.** No.

Chapter 6 1. Black and white. **2.** Yes. Yes. Yes. Yes. **3.** Seven. Seven. **4.** Seven. Seven. **5.** Zero. Zero. No. **6.** No. No. **7.** No. **8.** Four. **10.** A possible solution is to position the rooks on the main diagonal. **11.** The rook will move as if on a staircase: up-right-up-right. **12.** Yes on the first; no on the second one. **13.** The rook's paths will be as follows:1: a8xh8xh2 2: h5xh2xb2xb7 3: h3xf3xf5xd5xd7xb7 4: "staircase" up-left-up-left. 5: "spiral" up-right-down-left 6: a4xa1xh1xh8xb8xb2xf2xf6xe6xe7xc7xc5x g5xg3 **14.** The rook's paths will be as follows: 1: h5-d5 2: g1-g6 3: e7-b7 4: h1-h8 5: a8-h8-h7 6: h4-d4-d6 **15.** The rook's paths will be as follows: 1: h3-d3-d1-f1 2: c1-c4-a4-a3 3: h8-f8-f7-d7-d8-b8-b7-a7-a5-h5-h3-a3-a1-h1 4: b8-b7-f7-f8-h8-h5-c5-c3-h3-h1-a1-a6 5: a8-a6-c6-c7-d7-d8-f8-f7-h7-h5-f5-f3-h3-h1-b1-b2 6: h2-f2-f3 and then "staircase" left-up-left-up. **16.** The rook's paths will be as follows: 1: a3-b3-b4-e4-e1-c1 2: a4-a1-c1-c2-d2-d3-e3-e5-d5-d6-c6-c8-a8 3: b8-b7-a7-a3-b3-b1-f1-f2-g2-g3-h3-h7-f7-f5-d5 4: a1-d1-d7-f7-f5-h5-h3-f3-f1-h1 5: h1-h4-b4-b6-d6-d8-f8-f6-h6-h8 6: h1-f1-f2-c2-c6-h6-h8-a8-a1-b1 **17.** 1: ♖a7 2: ♖a8 3: ♖f8 4: ♖b5 5: ♖h6 6: ♖e1 **18.** 1: 1 ♖h2 ♖a2 2 ♖xa2 2: 1 ♖a7 ♖e7 2 ♖xe7 3: 1 ♖h5 ♖e5 2 ♖xe5 4: 1 ♖g7 5: 1 ♖h2 ♖f3 2 ♖g2 ♖f4 3 ♖g3 ♖e4 4 ♖f3 ♖e5 5 ♖f4 ♖d5 6 ♖e4 ♖d6 7 ♖e5 ♖c6 8 ♖d5 ♖c7 9 ♖d6 ♖b7 10. ♖c6 ♖b8 11 ♖c7 ♖a8 12 ♖b7 ♖b8 13 ♖xb8 6: 1 ♖c2 ♖b1 2 ♖c3 ♖b2 3 ♖d3 ♖c2 4 ♖d4 ♖c3 5 ♖e4 ♖d3 6 ♖e5 ♖d4 7 ♖f5 ♖e4 8 ♖f6 ♖e5 9 ♖g6 ♖f5 10 ♖g7 (10. ♖g8 works as well) 10...♖f6 11 ♖g8! (but not 11 ♖h7?? ♖g6 12 ♖g7 ♖xg7) 11...♖f5 12 ♖g6! ♖e5 13 ♖f6 ♖e4 14 ♖f5 ♖d4 15 ♖e5 ♖d3 16 ♖e4 ♖c3 17 ♖d4 ♖c2 18 ♖d3 ♖b2 19 ♖c3 ♖b1 20. ♖c2 ♖a1 21 ♖b2 ♖b1 22 ♖xb1.

Chapter 7 1. Light-square bishops travel on light squares. Dark-square bishops travel on dark squares. **2.** Dark squares. Light squares. **3.** Yes. Yes. **4.** No. No. **5.** No. No. **6.** Yes, a black bishop can. No. **7.** Yes, if they are same-colored bishops. Yes. **8.** Yes. **9.** Yes. **10.** No. **11.** No. Bishops can't jump over other pieces. **12.** White light-square bishop. White dark-square bishop. Black dark-square bishop. Black light-square bishop. **13.** In one. In four. **14.** A possible position: all bishops are either on the same rank or file. **15.** 1: Yes. 2: No. 3: No. 4: No. **16.** The bishop's paths will be as follows: 1: e5xb8xa7 2: b3xd1xg4 3: b6xd8xg5xc1 4: d4xe3xf2xg3xh4xd8xa5 5: g1xh2xc7xa5xe1xh4xe7xa3xc1xh6xg7

6: b7xa6xf1xh3xd7xa4xd1xh5xf7xa2xb1xh7 **17.** The bishop's paths will be as follows: 1: c3-a5 2: d5-a2 3: d2-h6 4: b5-e8 5: c3-h8 6: f5-c8 **18.** The bishop's paths will be as follows: 1: a2-b3-a4-b5-a6-b7-a8 2: b2-c1-d2-e1-h4-g5-h6-g7-h8 3: h2-g3-h4-g5-h6-f8-e7-d8-c7-b8-a7 4: c6-a4-c2-d3-e2-f3-h1 5: h3-g4-h5-e8-d7-c8-a6-c4-d5-e4 6: b1-c2-d1-e2-f1-h3-f5-e4-d5-c4-a6-c8-d7-e8-f7-g8-h7 **19.** 1: ♖d4 or ♖e5 2: ♖b7 or ♖g3 3: ♖a8 or ♖h1 4: ♗b7 5: ♗e5 6: ♗b5 **20.** 1: ♖d4 2: ♖g4 3: ♖e8 4: ♗c7 5: ♗c3 6: ♗e4 **21.** 1: ♖xd5 2: ♖xd3 3: ♖xh8 4: ♖xh5 5: ♖xa8 6: ♗xc7 **22.** 1: ♖h3 2: ♖d8 **23.** 1: ♖a5 2: ♖h1 **24.** The white piece will follow these paths: 1: ♗c3-a5-d8-f6-h8 2: ♗d2-a5-d8-e7-f8-h6 3: ♗b2-c1-e3-b6-c7-b8 4: ♖b1-b2-c2-c3-e3-e2-h2-h4-g4-g5-f5-f8 5: ♖f1-f2-d2-d1-a1-a5-b5-b6 6: ♖d1-d3-h3-h6-g6-g8-f8-f7-a7-a6-b6-b4 **25.** The white piece will follow these paths: 1: ♗g1-e3-c1xb2 2: ♗c3-d2-c1-a3-c5-a7xb8 3: ♖h6-g6-g5-e5-e3xf3 4: the rook is moving "up the stairs" - right-up-right-up - and takes the bishop with the last move 5: ♗f8-h6-c1-b2xd4xe5 6: ♖f1 and then "up the stairs" up-left-up-left ; the rook takes the black bishops at the end of the path. **26.** 1: ♗f5 2: ♗b2 3: ♗b4 4: ♗e2 5: ♗b5 6: ♗b5 **27.** 1: ♗f4 2: ♗d4 3: ♗e5 4: ♗e4 5: ♖e2 6: ♖d1 **28.** 1: 1 ♗h6 ♗g7 2 ♗xg7 2: 1 ♗e8 ♗h7 2 ♗f7 3: 1 ♗h4 ♗h2 2 ♗g5 ♗g3 3 ♗h6 ♗h4 4 ♗g7 (4 ♗f8 works as well) 4...♗g5 5 ♗f8 (but not 5 ♗h8 ♗h6 and White loses the bishop) 5...♗h4 6 ♗h6! ♗g3 7 ♗g5 ♗h2 8 ♗h4 ♗g1 9 ♗g3 ♗h2 10. ♗xh2 4: 1 ♗g7 5: 1 ♖a7 6: 1 ♖c1 ♗a8 2 ♖c7.

Chapter 8 **1.** Both. **2.** Yes to all. **3.** Yes. Yes. **4.** No. No. **5.** No. **6.** In three. In eight. **7.** Seven. Seven. Zero **8.** Seven. Seven. Zero. **9.** Seven. Zero. Seven. **10.** Yes. No. **11.** A possible position is ♕a1, ♕b3, ♕c5, ♕d7 **12.** No. No. **13.** No. **14.** Yes. Yes. **15.** No. **16.** Black. **17.** 1: No. 2: Yes. **18.** The queen will follow these paths: 1: a1xa8xg2xc2 2: e4xa8xh8xb2 3: f2xf8xa3xh3xd7 4: g1xa7xh7xc2xc3 5: h1xa8xg8xg7xf6xe5xd4xc3xb2 6: a8xh8xh2xc2xc5xg5xg4xd7xf7xf1xe1 **19.** The queen's paths: 1: a2-b3 2: h8-h1 3: a1-h8 4: c4-f7 5: e6-h3 6: h2-b8-a8 **20.** 1: b1-c2-b3-a3 2: b1-c2-d1-e2-f1-h3-g4-h5-g6-h7-g8 3: f1-g2-b7-c8-f8 4: h2-g3-e1-c1-b2-b3-a4-b5-a6-b7-b8 5: f3-e3-d4-d5-c6-b6-a7-a8 6: b2-c1-g1-h2-h3-g4-g5-h6-g7-h8 **21.** 1: ♕c8, ♕h1 or ♕h6 2: ♕a7, ♕e4 or ♕h4 3: ♕g8, ♕h1 or ♕h2 4: ♕b6 5: ♕f4 6: ♕d7 **22.** 1: ♕e5 2: ♕e6 3: ♕c8 4: ♕c3 5: ♕d4 6: ♕b8 **23.** 1: ♕xd7 2: ♕xf7 3: ♕xf1 4: ♕xb5 5: ♖xe1 6: ♗xh8 **24.** 1: ♕f8 2: ♕b1 3: ♕h2 4: ♕e4 5: ♕a5 6: ♕a6 **25.** The white piece will follow these paths: 1: ♕b6-c7-c8-e8-g6-g7-h8 2: ♕b1-f5-a5 3: ♕a8-h1 4: ♕a2-e6-a6 5: ♗f6-h4-e1-d2-f4-h2 6: ♖c1-c7-h7 **26.** The queen's paths: 1: h1-a1-a3xb4xc5 2: a2-e6-b6xd4xc3 3: h1-e1xe2xe3 4: e7-e4-b4-a3xa2xa1 5: c1-b1-a2-b3-c3-g7-g8-d8xd7xe6xd5xd6 6: b7-c8-h8-h7-e4-d5-a5-a3-b2-c3-e1-h1xg2xe2 xf3xe3 **27.** 1: ♕e2 2: ♕h6 3: ♕g6 4: ♕f5 5: ♕c8 6: ♕a8 **28.** 1: ♕h8 2: ♕h2 3: ♕a8 4: ♕e7 5: ♕e5 6: ♕a1 **29.** 1: 1 ♕f3 2: 1 ♕a1 3: 1 ♕h3 4: 1 ♕f6 5: 1 ♖b1 6: 1 ♗d4 ♕c8 2 ♗a7 ♕b8 3 ♗xb8.

Chapter 9 **1.** Both black and white. **2.** Yes. Yes. **3.** Yes. **4.** The quickest path will take four moves. **5.** Six moves. **6.** In three moves for both. **7.** Two moves. **8.** Four moves. **9.** No. **10.** Yes. Two. **11.** From the center. **12.** No. **13.** 1: Yes 2: No. 3: No. 4: No. 5: Yes 6: No. **14.** The knight will follow these routes: 1: h1xg3xf5xe7 2: c4xb2xd1xf2xh3xg5 3: b3xa1xc2xe1xg2xh4xg6xh8 4: a8xc7xb5xa7xc8xe7 xf5xg7xh5 5: b1xa3xc2xb4xd3xc5xe4xd6xf5xe7xg6xf8xh7 6:g6xe5xf7xh6xf5xg3xe4xd2xb1xa3xb5 xc7xa8xb6xa4xb2 **15.** The knight's path: 1: d4-c6 2: f7-h8 3: f3-g1 4: f4-g2 5: f5-g3-h1 6: c7-e6-d8 **16.** The knight's path: 1: a3-c2-a1 2: h4-f3-g1-h3-f2-h1 3: c2-a3-b5-c7-a8-b6-a4-b2-d3-c1 4: f2-d1-b2-a4-b6-a8 5: f2-h3-g1-f3-h2-f1-e3-c2-a1-b3-c1-a2-c3-b5-c7-a8 6: a1-b3-d2-f1-g3-h5-g7-e8-c7-a8-b6-a4-b2-d3-e5-f7-h8 **17.** The knight's path: 1: ♘c3 2: ♘g3 3: ♘f6 4: ♘d2 5: ♘d4 6: ♘f5 **18.** 1: ♘e3 2: ♘d6 3: ♘d4 4: ♖e4 5: ♗e4 6: ♕a1 **19.** 1: ♘xb3 2: ♘xc3 3: ♘xg1 4: ♖xd1 5: ♗xh7 6: ♕xc7 **20.** 1: ♖h3 2: ♖a5 3: ♖a2 4: ♗f5 5: ♘g6 6: ♗b7 **21.** 1: ♗b2 2: ♘f2 3: ♖h8 4: ♗f6 5: ♖f4 6: ♘d4 **22.** The white piece's route: 1: ♘a3-c2-a1 2: ♘a1-b3-d2 3: ♘c7-e8-f6-e4-c3-a4-b2 4: ♖e1-e6-c6-c7-d7-d3 5: ♗f5-d7-a4-d1-e2-f1-

150

g2-a8 6: ♕d1-g4-d7-e7 **23.** The white piece's route: 1: ♘g6-f8-h7-f6xd5 2: ♘d2-e4-g5xh3 3: ♘c2-a3-b1xc3 4: ♘h1-g3xf5xe7xc8xb6xa4 5: ♖f1-f5-a5-a3xc3xd3 6: ♕d1-e2-e4-f5-f6-e7xb4xc4 **24.** 1: ♘h3 2: ♘d5 3: ♖f4 4: ♘e4 5: ♗f1 6: ♘d4 **25.** 1: ♗d4 2: ♗f5 3: ♗e5 4: ♘c6 5: ♖c4 6: ♘c5 **26.** 1: ♖e4 2: ♗e4 3: ♘d4 4: ♘e4 5: ♕d6 6: ♕e3.

Chapter 10 1. Both dark and light. **2.** Yes to all. **3.** Yes, from the starting position. **4.** No. **5.** Diagonally. **6.** In two. (one only for rook pawns) **7.** Yes. Yes. **8.** No. **9.** Two. **10.** Four. Two, four. **11.** No. **12.** Yes. **13.** No. **14.** No. **15.** A rook, a bishop, a knight, or a queen. **16.** No. **17.** No. No. **18.** The first rank; the eighth rank. **19.** No. **20.** No. **21.** No. **22.** No. **23.** 1: No. 2: Yes. 3: No. 4: Yes. 5: Yes. 6: No. **24.** The pawn' paths are as follows: 1: e2xd3xc4xb5 2: d2xe3xd4xe5 3: h2xg3xf4xe5xf6xg7 4: d2xe3xf4xg5xf6xe7xd8 5: Diagonally to the right 6: "Zigzag" **25.** The pawn's route: 1: e4-e5-e6-e7-e8 2: c8♘ (the pawn is promoted to a knight)-♘a7 3: a4-a5-a6-a7-a8♘-♘c7 4: e4-e5-e6-e7-e8♘-♘g7-♘h5 5: h4-h5-h6-h7-h8♕ (the pawn is promoted to a queen)-♕b8-♕a7-♕a2 6: c4-c5-c6-c7-c8♕-♕b8-♕a7-♕a2 **26.** 1: e5 2: c4 3: g7 4: ♘d5 5: ♗e3 6: ♗d7 **27.** 1: d3 2: e4 3: ♖a5 4: ♗d5 5: ♘d6 6: ♕a7 **28.** 1: de 2: dc 3: dc 4: ef 5: ♖xe6 6: ♘xc6 **29.** 1: e3 2: d4 3: ♘e3 4: ♗c4 5: ♘e3 6: ♕c2 **30.** 1: ♖a7 2: ♗b1 3: ♘d5 4: ♗c8 5: ♘h6 6: ♕c1 **31.** The white piece's path: 1: h4-h5-h6-h7-h8 2: e4-e5-e6-e7-e8 3: c4-c5-c6-c7-c8 4: ♘f2-d1-b2-c4 5: ♗b2-c1-d2-e1-h4-e7-f8 6: ♖a4-c4-c6-h6-h1 **32.** 1: 1 ♖d8 d1♕ 2 ♖xd1 2: 1 ♗d5 a2 2 ♗xa2 3: 1 ♘c3 d2 2 ♗xd2 4: 1 ♘f3 g1♕ 2 ♘xg1 5: 1 ♘c5 a2 2 ♘b3 a1♕ 3 ♘xa1 6: 1 ♘f3 b2 2 ♘d2 b1♕ 3 ♘xb1 **33.** 1: No. 2: No. 3: No. 4: Yes, c7 5: Yes, h5 6: Yes, e5 **34.** 1: No. 2: No. 3: No. 4: Yes. 5: Yes. 6: Yes.

Chapter 11 1. Both dark and light. **2.** Yes. Yes. Yes. **3.** Eight. Three. **4.** No. **5.** No. **6.** Queen is on the left; Bishop is on the right. **7.** Two. **8.** No. **9.** No. **10.** 1: Yes. 2: Yes. 3: No. 4: No. 5: Yes. 6: No. **11.** Every time the king takes the piece standing right next to it. **12.** The king's path: 1: d5-c6 2: e3-f2 3: f7-g8 4: f4-e3 5: d5-c6-b5 6: e2-d3-c4 **13.** The king's path: 1: h2-g3-f2-f1 2: e5-f4-g3-h2-g1-f1-e2-d3 3: a7-a6-a5-a4-a3-a2-b1-c2-d1-e1-f1-g2-h1 4: g8-f8-e8-d8-c8-b8-a7-b6-c6-d6-e6-f6-g6-h5-g4-f4-e4-d4-c4-b4-a3-b2-c1-d2-e1-f2-g1-h2 5: b1-c2-d1-e2-f1-g2-h3-g4-h5-g6-h7-g8-f8-e7-d6-e5-d4 6: g2-f3-e3-d4-e5-d6-c6-b7-a8 **14.** 1: ♔d5 2: ♔d3 3: ♔e3 4: ♔e4 5: ♔d5 6: ♔d4 **15.** 1: ♔d6 2: ♔e6 3: ♔e5 4: ♔e7 5: ♔f5 6: ♔c5 **16.** 1: ♔xa2 2: ♔xh2 3: ♔xe3 4: ♔xc4 5: ♔xf6 6: ♔xb5 **17.** 1: ♗c2 2: ♔a3 3: ♘d2 4: ♔d5 5: e7 6: b4 **18.** 1: ♔e4 2: ♔g4 3: ♔e5 4: ♔d4 5: ♔c2 6: ♔c7 **19.** The king's path: 1: d1-e2-f1-g2-h3-g4-h5-g6-h7 2: g1-f2-e1-d2-c1-b2 3: a4-a3-b2-c1-d1-e1-f1-g1-h1 4: h5-h4-h3-h2-g1-f1-e1-d1-c1-b1-a1 5: b1-a2-b3-c3-d3-e4-f4-g3-f2-e1 6: b2-c1-d2-e1-f2-g1-h2-h3-h4-g5-h6-g7-f8 **20.** The king's path: 1: a2-a3-a4-a5-a6xb7xc8xd7xe6 2: b1-c1-d1-e1-f1-g1-h2-g3xg4 and then each time the king takes the pawn closest to it. 3: h2-h3-h4-h5-g6-f7-e6-e5xe4xe3 4: d8-c8-b7-b6-b5-a4-b3-c3-d4-d5xd6xe5 5: g2-f3-e4-d5-c6-b7xb8 then each time the king takes the pawn closest to it. 6: a2-a3-a4-a5-a6-b7xc8 and the king takes all the pawns along c-file. **21.** 1: ♔b7 2: ♖g8 3: ♔b8 4: ♗h4 5: ♘c5 6: ♕f8 **22.** 1: 1 ♔c6 2:1 ♔h6! f5 2 ♖g5 f4 3 ♔xf4 3: 1 ♔c7 4: 1 ♔h7 ♖h8 2 ♔xh8 5: 1 ♔g6 6: 1 ♔g7 **23.** 1: No. 2: No. 3: No. 4: No. 5: Yes 6: Yes.

Chapter 12 1. 1: Yes. 2: Yes. 3: No. 4: No. **2.** 1: No. 2: No. 3: No. 4: Yes. 5: Yes. 6: Yes. **3.** 1: ♖h8+ 2: ♗g6+ 3: e7+ 4: ♘e6+ 5: ♕b4+ 6: ♕a1+ **4.** 1: 1 ♖d8+ and after the black king's move 2 ♖xh8 2: 1 ♘c3+ then 2 ♖xc7 3: 1 ♗e4+ and 2 ♗xa8 4: 1 ♘e6 and 2 ♘xc7 5: 1 e4+ then 2 ef 6: 1 ♕a2+ followed by 2 ♕xg8 **5.** 1: ♖xc8 2: ♔b2 3: ♗g8 4: ab 5: ♗g2 6: ♔c5 **6.** 1: ♖e1+ 2: ♖c5+ 3: ♗c4+ 4: ♗f8+ 5: ♕a5+ 6: g4+.

Chapter 13 1. A checkmate is better than a check. It's better to give checkmate than capture the queen. **2.** Yes. **3.** For example, White: ♔a3, ♖d1; Black: ♔a1 **4.** 1: Yes. 2: Yes. 3: Yes. 4: No. 5: No. 6: No. **5.** 1: Yes. 2: Yes. 3: No. 4: No. 5: No. 6: Yes. **6.** 1: Stalemate 2: Stalemate 3: Stalemate 4: Checkmate 5: Checkmate 6: Checkmate **7.** 1: ♖h8# 2: ♖h6# 3: ♖g1# 4: ♖a8# 5: ♖h7# 6: ♖b8# **8.** 1: ♗e4# 2: ♗d5# 3: ♗e8# 4: ♗c3# 5: ♗g6# 6: ♗f8# **9.** 1: ♕e8# 2: ♕g2# 3: ♕a8# 4: ♕e7# 5: ♕h6# 6: ♕e7# **10.** 1: ♘c7# 2: ♘g3# 3: ♘c4# 4: ♘xf6# 5: ♘c4# 6: ♘f6# **11.** 1: b7# 2: fg# 3: d7# 4: c8♕# 5: g4# 6: f8♘# **12.** 1: ♔c2# 2: ♗f7# 3: ♗e6# 4: hg# 5: ♘c7# 6: ♗e4# **13.** 1: White checkmates ♕h5# 2: White checkmates ♕xf7# 3: White checkmates ♘f6# 4: Black checkmates ♘f3# 5: Black checkmates ♗xf2# 6: Black checkmates ♕xf2#.

Chapter 14 **1.** 1: 1 ♗f6 g5 2 fg#. 2: 1 ♗b5 a1♕ 2 b4#. 3: 1 ♘b5 (but not 1 ♘e8? b5 2 ♘c7+ ♗xc7) and after any move of the black bishop 2 ♘c7#. 4: 1 ♗b2 a4 2 ♘c4#. 5: 1 ♗b7 and following the black bishop's retreat 2 ♗xc7#. 6: 1 ♔b8 and 2 ♘c7# is unavoidable. **2.** 1: 1...c5, then 2...b6#. 2: 1...♘g5 2 h7 ♘f7#. 3: 1...♔e6 and 2...f5#. 4: 1...♔c4 2 b5 ab#. 5: 1...bc♖ 2 ♔a3 ♖a1#. 6: 1...♗f4+ 2 ♗xf4 h3#. **3.** 1: 1 ♖h7+ ♔xh7 2 ♕g7#. 2: 1 ♖a6+ ba 2 ♖b8#. 3: 1 ♖h8+ ♘xh8 2 ♖g7#. 4: 1 ♖a6 ba (the reply to any move by the black bishop is 2 ♖xa7#) 2 b7# (by Paul Morphy.) 5: 1 ♖e7+ ♘xe7 2 ♘f6#. 6: 1 ♖xa7+ ♔xa7 2 ♖a5#. **4.** 1: 1...♗b3+ 2 ♔xb3 ♕b1#. 2: 1...♗a3+ 2 ♔xa3 (if the king retreats to the first rank, then 2...♕xc1#) 2...♕b4#. 3: 1...♗b2 2 ♗xb4 (otherwise 2...♕a2#) 2...♕a1#. 4: 1...♗e3+ 2 ♕xe3 (or 2 ♕f2 ♗xf2#) 2...♕f1#. 5: 1...♗f3+ 2 ♕xf3 (or 2 ♕e2 ♗xe2#) 2...♕e1#. 6: 1...♗e3+ 2 ♖xe3 ♖d1#. **5.** 1: 1 b7+ and 2 ♕a7# is inevitable. 2: 1 g4+ ♔xg4 2 ♕g6#. 3: 1 b4+ ♔xb4 2 ♗d2#. 4: 1 g3+ ♔xg3 2 ♘g2#. 5: 1 b4 ab 2 ♗b2#. 6: 1 d4 ed (no other reply would save Black either) 2 ♕e6#. **6.** 1: 1...♘b3+ 2 ab ♖a8#. 2: 1...♘g3+ then 2...♕xg2#. 3: 1...♘b3+ 2 ab ♕a3#. 4: 1...♘d3+ 2 ed f2#. 5: 1...♘c2+ 2 ♖xc2 ♖b1#. 6: 1...♘g3 2 hg (otherwise 2...♕h2) 2...♕h4#. **7.** 1: 1 ♕xh7+ ♔xh7 2 ♖h1#. 2: 1 ♕d5+ ♔xd5 (if 1...♔b8, then 2 ♕b7#) 2 ♖c8#. 3: 1 ♕a6+ ba (or 1...♔a7 2 ♕xa7#) 2 ♗c6#. 4: 1 ♕a7+ ♕xa7 2 ♘c7#. 5: 1 ♕g6 hg 2 ♖h8#. 6: 1 ♕h5+ gh 2 ♖h6#. **8.** 1: 1...♕xg1+ 2 ♔xg1 ♖b1#. 2: 1...♕xa2+ 2 ♔xa2 ♖a7#. 3: 1...♖h1+ 2 ♔xh1 ♖f1#. 4: 1...♕a1+ 2 ♔xa1 ♖xa1#. 5: 1...♖f1+ 2 ♖xf1 ♖e2#. 6: 1...♕f3 2 ef (otherwise 2...♕g2#) 2...♖xe1#. **9.** 1: 1 ♕e4+ ♗xe4 2 ♗xe4#. 2: 1 ♕a6+ ♔xa6 (otherwise 2 ♕c8#) 2 ♗c8#. 3: 1 ♕xg7+ ♗xg7 2 ♗xg7#. 4: 1 ♕g7+ ♗xg7 2 ♗xg7#. 5: 1 ♕xf7+ ♔xf7 (if 1...♔h8, then ♕g7#) 2 ♗e6#. 6: 1 ♕xc6+ bc 2 ♗a6#. **10.** 1: 1...♖h6+ 2 gh g6#. 2: 1...♕xa2+ 2 ♘xa2 b5#. 3: 1...♕g4+ 2 ♔xg4 hg#. 4: 1...♕g2+ 2 ♔xg2 hg#. 5: 1...♘xd3+ 2 ed f2#. 6: 1...♘c3+ 2 ♕xc3 b5#. **11.** 1: 1 ♕xh7+ ♘xh7 2 ♘g6#. 2: 1 ♕b8+ ♖xb8 2 ♘c7#. 3: 1 ♖g5+ fg (or 1...♔h8 2 ♕g7#) 2 ♘h6#. 4: 1 ♖b8+ ♖xb8 2 ♘c7#. 5: 1 ♖xh7+ ♕xh7 2 ♘g6#. 6: 1 ♕g7+ ♕xg7 2 ♘h6#. **12.** 1: 1 ♖xh7+ and 2 ♕g7#. 2: 1 ♖c8+ ♖xc8 (or 1...♔xc8 2 ♘c7#) 2 ♕e7#. 3: 1 ♘b6+ ab 2 ♕a6#. 4: 1 ♖b8+ and inevitably 2 ♕xa7#. 5: 1 ♖h5+ gh 2 ♕f6#. 6: 1 ♖xd6+ ed (or 1...cd 2 ♕a5#) 2 ♕g5#. **13.** 1: 1...♖h3+ 2 gh ♖h2#. 2: 1...♘d3+ 2 ed ♕e7#. 3: 1...♕g1+ and 2...♘f2#. 4: 1...♖h8+ 2 ♔xh8 0-0-0#. 5: 1...♕h1+ and 2...♖c1#. 6: 1...♘c3+ 2 bc ♗a3#. **14.** 1: 1 ♕xa7+ ♔xa7 2 ♖a5#. 2: 1 ♕d8+ ♔xd8 (if 1...♔b7, then 2 ♕xb8) 2 ♖xb8#. 3: 1 ♖a8+ ♔xa8 2 ♘c8#. 4: 1 ♖h7+ ♔xh7 2 ♘f7#. 5: 1 ♕f8+ ♖xf8 (or 1...♔xf8 2 ♖h8#) 2 ♘e7#. 6: 1 ♕c8+ ♖xc8 2 c7#. **15.** 1: 1...♕xg3+ (or 1...♖xg3+) 2 hg ♗xg3#. 2: 1...♘ef3+ (or 1...♘df3+, either knight can check) 2 gf ♘xf3#. 3: 1...♘f3+ and 2...♖xf2#. 4: 1...♖xh2+ 2 ♔xh2 hg#. 5: 1...♕xf1+ 2 ♘xf1 ♘f2#. 6: 1...♘c4+ 2 ♗xc4 ♖e3#. **16.** 1: 1 ♘f6+ gf 2 ♗xf7#. 2: 1 ♗h5+ ♖xh5 2 ♕g6#. 3: 1 ♕g6+ hg 2 ♗xg6#. 4: 1 ♖xe6+ fe (or 1...♗e7 2 ♕xe7#) 2 ♗g6#. 5: 1 ♕xh7+ ♔xh7 2 ♖h5#. 6: 1 ♖h5 gh (otherwise 2 ♕xh7#) 2 ♕f6#.

Chapter 15 **1.** 1: 1 ♔b2 2: 1 ♔g2 3: 1 ♖b1+ 4: 1 ♗c4+ 5: 1 0-0-0 6: 1 g4+ and 2 ♕xa8 **2.** 1: 1...♔b7 2: 1...♔g7 3: 1...♖e8 4: 1...e4+ 5: 1...♘d5+ 6: 1...♗f6 and 2...♗xa1 **3.** 1: 1 ♖xh7+ ♔xh7 (or 1...♔g8 2 ♕xg6#) 2 ♕xg6+ ♔h8 3 ♕h7#. 2: 1 ♖h8+ ♔xh8 2 ♕h4+ ♔g8 3 ♕h7#. 3: 1 ♕h8+ ♔xh8 2 ♗f6 ♔g8 3 ♘e7#. 4: 1 ♕d8+ ♔xd8 2 ♗g5+ ♔c7 (or 2...♔e8 3 ♖d8#) 3 ♗d8#. 5: 1 ♗g4+ ♔xg4 2 ♖xh6+ gh 3 ♗f7# (inspired by the game Vaccaroni vs Mazzochi, Rome, 1891) 6: 1 ♘e6+ ♕xe6 (1...de and 1...♖xe6 lead to the same variations. If 1...fe, then 2 ♕f6#) 2 ♕h6+ ♔xh6 (otherwise 3 ♕f8#) 3 ♗f8#.